Come See the Light

A Future History Novel

By

Norman Luce

Cover art by Rebecacovers

ISBN: 978-0-578-38226-5

Table of Contents:

Authors Note & Acknowledgments

This future history novel's underlying hypothesis or speculation was inspired by a short screenplay co-written with a friend of mine. The screenplay was produced for the San Jose 48 Hour Film Project of 2016. To this day, it remains one of my proudest artistic achievements and one of my fondest memories as a filmmaker. Initially, my friends and I intended to write and produce a feature-length film based on our short script. However, various circumstances interfered with the task, and it was decided to put the idea on hold. It wasn't until the COVID-19 pandemic that I abandoned the idea of a screenplay and decided to write the story as a novel.

I mention this because, while this book was written by me, it was edited by many of my family & friends who also provided insights into the story's potential trajectory and some of the details. Thus, it would be inappropriate not to give credit where credit is due. This book is the result of my creativity combined with the guidance and perspectives of many people in my life I feel fortunate to know. To those who participated in the 48 Hour Film Project with me that year, I hope you enjoy the new direction I have taken our story and that it also reminds you of fond memories. To those who helped me craft this book, I thank you for your guidance from the bottom of my heart. I hope you will be as proud of this story as I am.

I would especially like to extend my deepest gratitude to Kamilla Bylina, the creator of the animated commercial for this book. Her tireless efforts and incredible talent shine through in her stunning creation, and I thank her for taking a chance on this project and creating the most beautiful work of animation I have ever seen. I wish her all the best and I hope the commercial paves the way towards a bright future for us both. Thank you, Kamilla. You are a true artist in every sense of the word.

Forward

The first interaction I had with Norman Luce was through a series of emails explaining what the 48 Hour Film Project entailed. We were introduced by a mutual theater friend in 2016. I was 5 years into my nursing career and was just barely getting into the world of community theater as a hobby to de-stress. Since then, I have been involved in multiple film projects of Norman's Dragon Farm Productions. It has been a pleasure to be part of something that has challenged me and helped foster the creative version of myself that had been latent for quite some time.

"Come See the Lights" was the name of our first 48 Hour Film Project together. This project was awarded "Best Cinematography" which is one of the aspects that made our sleepless weekend of work feel like a success. The excitement I felt while working on this film was akin to how thrilled I was to hear that Norman was turning this screenplay into a full-length novel. Norman did a fantastic job adding more layers of this tale than I could ever imagined possible. This story was a painful yet important reminder of how showing empathy can be the right thing to do yet the difficult choice to make. Everyone wants to be a hero, but no one wants to suffer the pressure points that made them that way.

I'm grateful to Norman for taking a chance on me and trusting me with bringing this story to life – both in film and in writing. Connections like this have the power to inspire us to learn and do better, despite the daily turmoil that occurs. I appreciated how the story also made me reflect on the importance of building trust in yourself. We don't always see the potential and brightness in ourselves and there are times when we barely see a flicker; however, this does not mean that it is not there. May this story remind you that seeing the light in others, as well as yourself, is a choice that you can always make.

Sarah Liz Amoroso
a.k.a.
Maya

For my grandmothers, my sisters, and my
niece.

The war raged
onward
争战如火如荼

But there was no
escaping
无所逃脱

Great change in The
Wave
洪涛掀起巨变

Prelude

The Wave

May 15, 2037 – 2:16 PM, Pacific Time

Dr. Samuel Clarke, Ph.D., a specialist in electrophysics, stood before his creation. He stared at the pulsing machine before him, a giant metallic sphere with hexagon-shaped attachments all around. It stood on a large pedestal with thick cables loosely strung around like robotic tentacles. Even with the thick transparent shield, he could still feel the heat of the white light emanating from its atomic core. He was reminded of a quote from Fredrick Nietzsche: "Whoever fights monsters should see to it that in the process he does not become a monster."

Suddenly, his best friend and colleague, Professor Mae Douglass, burst into the room with a scrap of paper in her hand.

She paused and then said, almost in a whisper, "It's happening."

Professor Douglass handed the paper to Dr. Clarke, who read it carefully. Once he finished reading, he crumpled it up and threw it onto the floor.

"Those idiots!" he said. "How could they do this to us?"

"Listen," replied Douglass, "I'm scared too, but there's nothing we can do about it. We have to get out of here."

"And go where? Once they go through with it, there will be nowhere we can escape!"

Professor Douglass looked disheartened, struggling to find the words.

"I'm sorry," she said, "but there's nothing we can do."

Then, as if lightning struck his mind, Dr. Clarke came to a drastic realization.

"Yes, there is," he said. "The Wave. It can work. I know it will."

Professor Douglass, realizing the situation, suddenly became a bit wary of her companion.

"No, you can't be serious. Think of the disasters it will cause, the lives that will be lost!"

"I know," replied Dr. Clarke, "but at least there will still be a world for those who are left."

Professor Douglas's heart sank. She could not fathom what was becoming of the man she admired. Even so, she knew he was still somewhere in there, somewhere deep inside. With gentle firmness, she placed her hands on his shoulders, and looked right into his eyes.

"Listen to me," she said softly, "the world has made its choice. It's not our place to interfere. Let's just find some solace in the little time we have left together."

Dr. Clarke gazed into his companion's eyes. They were filled with such sincerity… and hope. He could not help himself but tear up a little at the beautiful sight before him.

"Okay," he said, "let's go."

With that, Professor Douglass smiled and went straight out the door. She stopped on the other side and waited for Dr. Clarke to join her.

"Come on," she said.

Slowly, Dr. Clarke stepped closer to the door, only to stop at the last moment. He stared at his companion as if he was saying good-bye for the last time, "I'm sorry, Mae," he said, then slammed the safe-like door, spinning the locking wheel to secure himself inside.

Professor Douglass bolted for the door, but it was too late as the sound of the door lock echoed all through the dark hallway on her side. Furiously, she banged on the door, cursing Dr. Clarke for his selfishness. She pleaded with him through the intercom to stop and leave with her, but it was too late. His vision of the future without immediate intervention was both clear and terrifying. Realizing her efforts were fruitless, and the eminent danger she could be in, Professor Douglass fled the building.

Dr. Clarke walked over to his desk and sat before his computer with dual monitors. He pressed a button and a transparent dome encompassed him at his desk.

"Pulse shield initiated" said a monotone voice from his computer speakers.

Dr. Clarke typed in a series of codes into his computer. Within seconds the left monitor displayed a hacked security camera feed of the Pentagon. Just as Dr. Clarke had feared, the launch was inevitable. He observed as the men in suits confirmed the last security check before preparing to push the button. At the same time, Dr. Clarke continued to input codes into his computer. On the right monitor, the words "Initiate Project Edison: Y / N" appeared on the screen. He hesitated, before choosing the key to punch.

"May they see the light of truth, someday."

With great pride and no regret, Dr. Clarke pushed the "Y" button on the keyboard.

"Project Edison has been initiated," said the computer voice. "T-minus 5...4...3...2...1."

Suddenly, the great sphere roared like a race car engine revving at its highest possible speed. The vibrations shook the very floor of Dr. Clarke's office like an earthquake. Without warning, the sphere let out a blinding burst of light, shooting across the room like a ribbon of water from a fire hydrant. The shock of its sudden burst nearly destroyed the whole room with hurricane force. Dr. Clarke and his computer remained untouched, thanks to the protection of the dome.

Meanwhile, outside, Professor Douglass was preparing her horse for the journey ahead. It was rather fortuitous she'd been on her afternoon ride when she received the news. As she checked the saddle bags, she saw the ribbon of light emanating from where she'd just departed. The Wave looked like a tsunami, a white translucent current shimmering in the dusky light as it flew over her head beyond the horizon.

As the Wave passed over the town below, Professor Douglass could see all the lights go out. Sparks flew from power lines as The Wave glided overhead. Cars suddenly stopped in their lanes, refusing to start up again. People's phone conversations were cut short as they lost all power. Some of the phones even exploded in small bursts of sparks.

As Professor Douglass looked farther, she noticed an airplane passing over the town. For a moment, she felt a terrible pain in the pit of her stomach. Which only grew as she watched the plane suddenly dive and disappear beyond the horizon. She had known this would happen, knew full well of the countless lives that Dr. Clarke's actions would cost.

She then looked back at the laboratory where she had been standing with Dr. Clarke not five minutes ago.

"Good-bye, Samuel."

With that, Professor Douglass mounted her horse and rode away.

Dr. Clarke watched on his protected computer screen as the feed from the Pentagon flashed an error message—surely this meant the launch was avoided—just seconds before the feed went dead. In a contemplative manner, he opened his desk drawer and carefully pulled out a small glass, a bottle of expensive Scotch, and a revolver.

He punched a few more commands on his keyboard.

"Hibernation mode: initiated," said the computer voice. A moment later, the computer shut down, allowing the pulse shield to retract.

As carefully as possible, he poured himself some Scotch and raised his glass.

"For Humanity!"

Dr. Clarke took the time to enjoy his drink. He then placed the glass on his desk and picked up the revolver. He opened the cylinder and saw a single bullet inside, just as he always kept it. Dr. Clarke closed the cylinder, pulled back the hammer, aimed the barrel under his chin, and placed his finger on the trigger.

His last thought was his favorite memory with his lover.

(Copy of the last known State of the Union from former President Byran Smallpockets. Created and copied with typewriters on loan from The Smithsonian Institute. Distributed to all major military bases and state capitals by The Dragoons, 1st Cavalry Regiment of Fort McNair, Greenleaf Point, Washington D.C.)

December 24, 2037

My Fellow Americans,

At the time of this writing, our U.S. Navy sailing vessel envoys have returned from coastal Europe, South America, Africa, and Asia. They report that the Calamity exists globally. Your Federal Government has no means of restoring electrical power. We have no means of confronting the rise of widespread disease and famine. We have no means of dealing with the reported looting, rioting, and civil unrest that is raging throughout our great nation.

Our top scientific investigators have studied the Calamity to great extent. According to their findings, by some means we cannot identify, their consensus is, and I quote: "The laws of electrophysics have been completely rewritten, to the point that all forms of non-biological electricity can no longer be generated or replicated." While the Federal Government has contingency plans in place for events such as massive power outages, they were drafted under the impression that power would eventually be restored. The Federal Government has no plan in place to function as it has in the 21st century without electrical power.

Therefore, the Federal Government is hereby dissolved. All governing authority is vested in whatever civilian organizations exist locally. All members of the US Military are directed to provide such assistance as they can to local authorities.

My thoughts are with you all in the hope that humanity will prevail. I hereby resign from the office of President after decades of service to my country. It has been an honor. I thank you all. Good luck!

Byran Smallpockets
The Last President of the United States

1

Forty-Seven Years Later

Spring, 2084, late morning

Maya admired the gorgeous view from her favorite spot on the hill, overseeing the lush landscape. The aroma of the fresh air complimented the sounds of birds singing as they flew by. She passed the time by sharpening a nearby stick with her favorite knife, as she had done many times before. *This will make an excellent spear,* she thought to herself, which is just what she needed now. Down the hill was a creek, where lots of game stopped for a drink. There, Maya would catch dinner for herself and the whole family. Maybe, if she was lucky, enough to share with the whole village.

Nineteen years old and a natural athlete, Maya stood just under six feet tall and towered over most of the other teens in her village. Her thick, smooth, dark hair seemed to always stay in place; perfectly parted and hanging behind her shoulders.

Her brown eyes shined like Tiger's Eye, especially during the day. Her tanned skin complemented her favorite jacket, which she had lined with pockets just about everywhere, including the sleeves. Her partial Thai heritage gave her a smooth complexion, with a smile that could put you at ease with its warmth. But make no mistake: if she must, she will take anyone down without a second thought, especially if they threaten anyone she loves.

Just then, Maya heard a noise coming from behind her. She tossed aside the stick and hopped up from her seated position. Swiftly, she rotated her knife and took a fighting stance, ready to defend herself.

"Maya?" cried a tiny voice.

A small figure appeared through the trees. It was Charlie, her younger brother. Maya let out a sigh of relief and sheathed her knife.

"Hey there, buddy," she replied in a welcoming tone.

Charlie ran straight to Maya and hugged her. Maya scooped him up and spun him around through the air as he giggled.

"What are you doing out here?" asked Maya.

"Dougie sent me to get you," replied Charlie.

"Then let's get going."

With Charlie in her arms, Maya headed back towards the village.

"Don't move!" said a terrible voice behind them. "Turn around!"

Maya froze in place, holding Charlie close. He buried his face into her shoulder.

"What's going on?" whispered Charlie.

"Don't worry," replied Maya, "it's all right."

"I said turn around!"

Carefully, Maya obliged. Turning around to face the mysterious voice, she was confronted by what looked like a vagabond: a scruffy-looking person with long, unkempt hair. Clothed in dirty rags barely holding together. Although, that was hardly as worthy of Maya's attention as the gun the stranger pointed at them.

"Take it easy," said Maya in a calming voice.

"Shut up!"

Maya held onto Charlie as tightly as she could, ready to run with him in her arms the second she was able.

"Give me the kid," the stranger demanded.

Charlie tightened his grip around Maya.

"Now look—" replied Maya,

"I said give me the fucking kid!" The stranger was growing more agitated by the second.

"Okay, okay, please calm down," said Maya.

The stranger pulled back the hammer, aiming the weapon directly at Maya, seemingly ready to fire at a moment's notice.

Maya whispered into Charlie's ear.

"Listen to me. I'm going to put you down. When I do, I want you to run for the creek and don't look back, understand?"

Charlie was too petrified to answer.

"Tell me you understand," whispered Maya.

"Okay," replied Charlie.

The stranger grew more impatient.

"Goddamn it, I won't tell you again!"

Slowly, carefully, Maya placed her younger brother on the ground. Suddenly, he bolted straight towards the creek. Maya stood there and watched her little brother run. The stranger stood there for a moment, wondering what to do next. After a few seconds, the stranger decided to give chase, and ran after Charlie.

Once the stranger was a few feet away from Maya, she picked up the stick with the speed and agility of an otter and threw it hard and true. A split second later, the makeshift spear was deeply embedded in the stranger's leg, causing the stranger to tumble and crash down onto the ground. Maya sprinted over. By the time the stranger looked up and realized what was happening, and tried to aim the gun, Maya kicked it high into the air with such force that the stranger's fingers were broken. Maya picked up the gun a few feet from the struggling vagabond and looked inside the cylinder. Empty, just as she had suspected.

"Maya!" cried Charlie.

Maya looked up and saw her little brother running back towards her. She kicked the stranger in the face as hard as she could, and ran straight towards Charlie. She held him in a comforting embrace.

"You did great, Charlie," she said. "Good job." She carefully took Charlie's shoulders to face him.

"Now listen to me," she said, "I need you to go straight back to the village. I'll be right behind you, okay? Go directly to Dougie's."

"What are you going to do?" asked Charlie.

Maya took a quick look at the stranger, who was turning and writhing in pain on the ground.

"Don't worry! He can't hurt you. Just go straight to Dougie's, okay?"

"Okay," replied Charlie.

"Okay. I'll be right behind you, buddy."

Charlie headed back toward the village. Maya stayed behind and watched her brother run away. Once he was out of earshot, Maya stood up and walked towards the stranger, drawing her knife.

The stranger tried to pull out the makeshift spear, but there was too much pain. A moment later, Maya was standing over the stranger. She grabbed the spear with one hand and yanked it out with incredible force. The stranger screamed. She didn't flinch. She kicked the stranger in the ribs before kneeling down and holding her knife against the stranger's throat.

"Were you going to eat him?" asked Maya.

The stranger seemed unable to reply.

"Answer me!"

Maya pressed the blade harder to the stranger's neck.

With a face covered in blood and a trembling voice, the stranger let out a simple reply:

"Yes."

Maya was still for a moment.

"Please, don't kill me," begged the stranger

A noise from up the hill caught Maya's attention for a moment, causing her to ignore the stranger's pleas. She took her knife away, tore a piece of the strangers clothing off, and shoved it into the strangers' mouth. With a sudden force, she jammed her knife straight through the stranger's shoulder and withdrew it as quickly as it went in. After all that, she yanked the cloth out, stood, and left the stranger there.

As Maya walked down the path, cleaning her knife, and placing it back into its sheath, she turned her attention up the hill and saw what had caused the noise she noticed earlier. A large black bear was making its way towards the stranger, smelling the blood, and hearing the cries.

"Wait!" cried the stranger. "You can't leave me here! Wait!" She did not reply.

As Maya retreated from view, the stranger looked all around in total fear. As if on cue, a deep growl echoed in the distance. The stranger could only watch in terror as the great beast stepped closer.

The screams made Maya's stroll back to her village far less pleasant than usual.

2

Home

The village was built around an old ranch near Lake Shasta, California. Douglass Ranch (as it came to be known) consisted of fifteen acres, with a population of around fifty. At the end of the lot, close to the old road, stood a two-story farmhouse, which belonged to the Douglass family. Throughout the lot were old storage containers transformed into apartments, hand-built wooden cabins, and sturdy old tarps forming canopies and tents here and there.

Near the center of the village was a large circular tent like something from a traveling circus show. This was the village's multipurpose center: depending on the time of day, it was a classroom, a meeting hall, an amphitheater, or a banquet hall. In the far corner of the village was the community garden and livestock pens, with goats, pigs, chickens, and a few cows.

As the villagers went about their day, the village founder, Professor Mae Douglass, known locally as Dougie, hosted a class of young and invested students. Even well into her 70s with her silver hair, aged skin, and walking stick, Dougie carried herself with a youthful enthusiasm which contributed to her popularity among her community. Her grandmotherly anecdotes peppered her classes so much that some likened it to childhood storytime—appropriate, since she often hosted storytelling events for the younger children.

The nickname Dougie was a bit unusual for an old woman, but one she enjoyed. It was reminiscent of her own childhood, and how she referred to her father when she was little. It was her first word, and the ultimate result from trying to say "daddy." Overtime, the word "Dougie" stuck, and it became an unexpected and pleasant term of endearment in her family ever since.

Soon after dismissing her class for the day, she had sent little Charlie to find Maya for her. Now, as Charlie came running into the village, Dougie was nervous not to see Maya as well. She quickly grabbed her walking stick and waved at Charlie, who ran straight towards her and wrapped his arms around her leg.

"I was so scared!" he cried.

"Calm down, little one," said Dougie, "what's the matter?"

"There was a stranger who tried to hurt us."

Dougie kneeled to Charlie's level and took his shoulder. "Are you hurt?"

"No."

"Is Maya hurt?"

"No, she told me to come straight back here. She said she was right behind me."

Dougie looked up and, sure enough, there was Maya, being enthusiastically greeted by some of the village's dogs. She bent down and gave them all pats as they licked her face.

Dougie sent Charlie inside and made her way towards Maya.

"I'm glad to see you're all right," she said.

"Dougie," replied Maya, still patting one of the dogs.

"What happened?"

Maya explained her encounter with the stranger, who she referred to as a "man eater". This caused a bit of concern for Dougie, since those folks rarely roamed too close to their own home. Despite her fears, Maya assured her that even if there were more of them around, they wouldn't likely find their little neck of the woods. Maya had made certain of that.

Dougie's heart was heavy for a moment. She never found comfort in the idea of Maya taking a life, even when justified. Maya understood this concern all too well, and reassured Dougie that she merely incapacitated the stranger. Andre did the rest.

"Andre," asked Dougie?

"You know," replied Maya, "that big bear I sometimes see on my excursions."

"I'm surprised that creature hasn't attacked you yet. You may have inherited your grandfather's charm with animals, young lady, but that hardly makes you Dr. Doolittle, you know."

"Doctor who?"

Suddenly, a sharp burst of pain seemed to overtake Dougie's arm. Maya instantly grabbed her and gently struck a few spots with her thumb. Slowly, the pain dissipated.

"How did you do that?" asked Dougie.

"Pressure points," replied Maya, "you all right?"

"I'm fine, my dear."

Maya knew that was a bold-faced lie. Despite her Great-Aunt's reassurances, whatever was ailing her was getting worse. Seeing her in pain suddenly flashed a memory into Maya's mind. A memory of her mother; an ugly, uncomfortable one at that. Maya shook off that terrible feeling and helped Dougie towards the house.

"I'm sorry I didn't bring anything nice back with me today," she said.

"You made it home safe; that's enough for me," replied Dougie.

The two of them shared a friendly giggle as they made their way towards the house.

"Hey, Maya!" cried a voice from behind them.

Maya and Dougie turned around and were greeted by Joseph, Maya's friend, and the village's blacksmith—a handsome man in his mid-twenties with a farmer's strong build. His thin jacket billowed in the wind, along with his long chocolate brown hair, which was tied back into a messy ponytail. And his green eyes could be seen from miles away.

"Joseph, what can I do for you?" asked Maya.

"You have a second? I got something to show you," replied Joseph.

Maya gestured to Joseph to wait for a moment while she checked in with Dougie.

"Can you make it inside on your own?" she asked.

"I am perfectly capable of walking into my own house, young lady!"

After exchanging a friendly laugh, Dougie headed towards the door as Maya walked towards Joseph.

"What have you got for me?" she asked.

"I just finished the blade according to your specs."

Joseph pulled out a piece of cloth from his pouch. He unwrapped it and revealed a thin blade, about six inches long and one inch wide. It shone like silver in the sunlight.

"Wow," said Maya, "it's perfect!"

"It wasn't easy, let me tell you."

Maya picked up the shiny blade and scrutinized it. "Thank you so much."

"No worries," he replied. "What's it for?"

"It's for a little project of mine. A secret weapon. One I really could have used today."

Joseph was genuinely concerned for his friend's well-being, asking if she was okay. After reassuring her friend, Maya profusely thanked Joseph for his delightful craftsmanship. Before Joseph could say anything else, Maya turned and made her way quickly to the main house, her prize clutched close to her chest.

3

Solace Workshop

Night fell, and Maya retreated to her upstairs bedroom in the main house. She enjoyed the occasional solitude of her room: formerly the house's attic, it had plenty of space for her and her many hobbies.

Tonight, she was concentrating on her latest project: a hidden retractable blade. She recalled one of the older villagers talking about how he used to play an electronic game back in the Days of Power, his favorite one featured a character with a retractable blade for sneaky kills. Maya liked the idea of having a hidden weapon handy for emergencies, especially after dealing with that man-eater earlier. Now, with Joseph's fine-tuned blade, she could finally build one.

She recalled the older villager saying that the blade was stationary and could only retract from the wrist. Maya wondered how it would be more practical if she could fire the blade over a decent distance. It would certainly look much more impressive.

Maya took the custom blade, a ring, some wire, some leather straps, various bits of scrap metal, and a few springs, and got to work. Soon, she had a working prototype. It was crude and uncomfortable to wear, but it was a start. It just needed to be tested before it could be fine-tuned. She stuck a piece of paper with a quickly-drawn target onto the wall, and stepped back towards her workbench. It was an excellent twenty-five-feet across her room. She prepped the spring system, carefully aimed at the target, and flicked her wrist to activate the mechanism. In a flash, the blade shot out from her wrist and flew three feet before clattering onto the floor.

She sighed, and smiled. Undeterred, she returned to her workstation and continued to modify her design. As she looked through her many drawers for materials, she came across something she had almost forgotten: a light bulb. The old-fashioned glass orb had a wire filament inside, and was as mysterious to Maya, having been born well into The Wave's aftermath, as anything from fantasy.

She recalled some of Dougie's stories about the Days of Power. How things like lights and letters once ran on human-generated electricity. People once carried around mobile devices and relied upon them for just about everything.

Maya looked at the old bulb with a sense of wonder. She imagined how it must have looked when it was lit up. It must have been so bright and beautiful back then. Even though Maya had never seen a single electrical item powered on in her life, she longed to bear witness to its beauty, if only for a moment.

Her thoughts came to an abrupt halt at the sound of little footsteps running up the stairs to her room.

"Hey, Maya!"

She quickly placed the old bulb back inside the drawer, then turned and braced herself for the pounce. Charlie bolted across the room and leaped in for a big hug.

"Oh, you're getting so big," she said.

"The show is starting! Let's go see it!"

"Oh, right!" She'd nearly forgotten—how long had she been staring at that thing? "You go back downstairs and get your coat. I'll be down in a minute, okay?"

"I don't want to wear my coat."

"Hey, no arguments, now. You hear me?"

Charlie frowned a little.

"All right," he replied sulkily.

"Hey," said Maya, "no sass either, young man!"

Charlie did as he was told and headed back downstairs to get his coat. Maya picked up a small cloth and covered her contraption. Its progress would have to wait for a while. Right now, it was time to join the village for a bit of fun.

4

The Showstopper

Maya and Charlie arrived at the multipurpose area about five minutes after the show had begun. Tonight was a special treat, especially for the kids. Under the direction of Dougie, some of the villagers put together an old-fashioned shadow puppet play. A small fire illuminated a thin white screen from behind on stage. A few volunteers were operating puppets, handmade from paper and animal skins, between the fire and the sheet. Even in the orange glow of the flames, the colors of the puppets shone through.

Tonight's story was *The Clever Foxes*. This was a favorite among the village children, since the crafty kitsune made them gasp and laugh with their antics. They always cheered at the Inari spirit, a character from Japanese folklore who appeared in both human and fox form and sent the clever foxes as her messengers into the world. The shapeshifting creatures were rendered beautifully in light and shadow.

Dougie was sitting stage right, acting as narrator. Charlie joined the other children, who huddled together close to the stage, excited and awed. Maya sat with the other adults.

She loved the shadow puppet shows. They reminded her of Great-Auntie Dougie telling her stories in candlelight, with great conviction and enthusiasm, when she was little. Those precious memories held a dear space in her heart.

The show was going well, until Dougie reached the story of Miles "Tails" Prower, a plucky red fox with two tails whose best friend was a lightning-fast hedgehog.

The old lady was in the middle of narrating a pivotal moment in the story, when she quietly stopped for seemingly no reason. She looked down at her hand, which had been in pain earlier that day. The performers were stuck in place as they waited for Dougie to proceed. Maya looked on from her place in the audience, nervous at once.

A moment later, Dougie continued her narration as if she hadn't stopped. Then, a few minutes later, she stopped again. This time, the pain in her hand shot straight through her arm to her chest. The shock was so intense she fell off her chair and directly onto the floor, clutching her chest as if she were wrestling with a wild animal.

Maya bolted out of her seat and ran straight for Dougie. She leaped onto the stage and applied some of her pressure point techniques to Dougie's arm, but to no effect. It was as bad as she had feared.

"Doctor," cried Maya, "somebody get the doctor! Now!"

Some other adults did their best to calm down the children as the performers dropped their puppets and made their way towards Dougie. Within seconds, the village doctor, an older, kindly woman called Ramona, who had been observing the shadow play from the far side of the green, arrived onstage and quickly examined Dougie.

"Her pulse is weak," she said. "We need to get her inside. Help me carry her."

They brought her indoors and went about the business of fetching water and supplies. It would likely be a long night. On the little stage, forgotten and fluttering in the evening winds, a paper fox stirred.

5

Revelation

Maya woke the following morning with a start in an old lounge chair, located in the corner of Dougie's room. Carefully, she approached Dougie and examined her condition. Dougie's breathing was slow and seemed to be slightly hindered, but as far as Maya could tell, at the very least, she wasn't in pain. Feeling reassured for the moment, she stepped out of the bedroom and headed for the kitchen.

When she returned, Dougie was awake.

"Dougie?" She carefully approached her. "How do you feel?"

Dougie hesitated before proclaiming she was all right. Maya immediately retorted out of genuine concern.

"I told you before," she said, "whatever this is, it's getting worse. I want to help you."

"I know you do, my dear. You always have. Just like your mother."

Silence.

"I'm afraid," Dougie continued, "that my time on this Earth is coming to an end."

Maya didn't like where this was going, and discouraged Dougie from entertaining such an idea.

"It is inevitable, my dear," Dougie continued. "I'm sorry. There is no 'proper time,' only the time we have here and now. Even so, I am guilty of not taking the time to teach you the most important thing of your life."

Maya stared at Dougie with incredible curiosity.

"What are you talking about?" asked Maya.

"My dear," replied Dougie, "there is something I have needed to tell you for a long time. I had planned to tell you about this before my passing, and when you were old enough to understand. Now, that time has come, sooner than I had wished." She reached into her pocket and pulled out a small key.

"Go into my study. Use this key to open the center compartment of my desk. Bring me everything that's inside."

Maya took the key and did as she was asked. She made her way into Dougie's study and toward her desk in the corner. As she moved an old typewriter out of the way, she found the locked compartment and used the key to open it. Inside was an old manilla envelope, with a red string wrapped around a circle to keep it closed. Cautiously, Maya picked it up. Upon realizing there was nothing else inside the compartment, she closed it and took the envelope back to the bedroom.

Upon entering, Maya noticed a severe look on Dougie's face. The kind that she usually saw when she or her brother was in trouble. She suddenly felt a bit uneasy.

"Open it," said Dougie.

Maya carefully unwound the red string and opened the envelope. She reached in and pulled out the first piece of paper. It was a typewritten letter, addressed to her:

My dear Maya,

If you are reading this, then I am not long for this world. I have tried my best to prepare you for this day. You have been the light of my life, and I am incredibly proud of you. I am leaving you the house and all my worldly possessions. Do with them what you will.

Now, we come to the most important reason for this letter. For there is something I have always meant to tell you.

Many years ago, a man I considered my best friend, Dr. Samuel Clarke, invented a machine that would change the world. He called it "The Wave". A device capable of changing the laws of electrophysics, nullifying all non-biological electricity, indefinitely.

In the time before you were born, he sought to save humanity from itself. We were on the brink of our own annihilation. Humankind had grown too powerful: atomic weapons, germ warfare, corruption, misinformation, and overpopulation, it all brought us closer to extinction. Such was the ultimate outcome of The Third Great War.

The only way to save humanity, according to Dr. Clarke, was to remove its power, and remove it he did.

But the work is ongoing and requires occasional maintenance. The machine will work forever so long as it is kept in good condition. I have been taking it upon myself to accomplish this very task. Now, I must leave it in your capable hands.

On my last visit, I left behind clues for you to seek out on your first venture to the machine. With this letter, you will find the first clue to begin your journey.

You must ensure that these clues are returned or destroyed once they have served their purpose.

You will also find the instructions for operating the machine. They are written in my own cipher and require a key to decode, located at your ultimate destination.

This task I lay before you will not be easy, but I have the utmost confidence you can do it. Humanity must prove itself worthy of power once again. Consider this my dying wish.

All my love to you my dear,
Dougie

Maya stared in complete disbelief. Anger began to twist inside her.

"This isn't funny, Professor."

"I assure you, my dear, I am quite serious."

An awkward silence fell upon the room. Maya inspected the envelope further. As the letter stated, the first clue was inside. It was a sketch of a dragon statue. A single "X" was drawn beneath the dragon's hind leg. Written below the drawing was a single word: Yreka.

"There, you will find your next clue," said Dougie. "The next of many, until you reach your destination. The location of The Machine."

"Stop," said Maya. "You expect me to believe that you had a part in ending the Days of Power?"

"I expect you to believe whatever you want, my dear, but that is not relevant right now. All I am talking about is the truth and what needs to be done for humanity's sake."

"Why couldn't you just draw a simple map with an "X" on the destination, like they do in the stories? Why this weird scavenger hunt?"

"Because I could not risk it being discovered by anyone else. The location of The Machine could only be entrusted to those I deemed worthy."

Maya tossed the envelope onto the floor and paced frantically across the room. The prospect of the long journey ahead was not frightening to her, as she has ventured out into the wilds before, but never too far, and most certainly never for something as massive and far-fetched as this. *It was her, it was her, all those horrible stories, all those frightened people, the world going dark, it was her all along.* Maya wanted it all to be untrue; she wanted it to be a poorly timed joke or the ravings of a demented old woman. But she could see it in Dougie's eyes: she was dead serious.

"My dear," she said, "I've wanted nothing more than to ensure the best possible future for you. You don't know what it was like before the war. You were spared the horrors of what I had to live through: population decrease, uncontrollable sickness, nuclear fallout! This was our only escape! I am sorry for placing this responsibility on your shoulders now. I don't have a choice."

Maya suddenly wheeled on Dougie, her own hands balled into fists at her sides.

"Well, I do," she said. "I can ignore this whole thing and just chalk it up to you being out of your mind because of your heart attack last night. I'm not going to go on some childish treasure hunt so I can save the world, from you, fifty years too late. You expect me to just go along with this? Out of what, faith!?"

Silence.

"I don't," said Dougie. "You don't have to believe me, my dear. You must only do what you feel to be right."

Maya rolled her eyes.

"This is not how I wanted to tell you," Dougie continued, "but it is the truth, nevertheless. And the only way that you will ever know for sure is if you trust me and perform this task, as my dying wish. I promise you; I will be with you every step of the way."

Maya felt torn asunder. She loved her great-aunt profoundly. She wanted to believe the best of her. But how could she reconcile this story? And what would be the point if she did? She looked at the envelope she had thrown onto the floor, picked it up, and slid the letter back inside.

"Let me think about it," she said, softly.

"Of course, my dear," replied Dougie. Her eyes were searching, and Maya knew there was hurt in them. She could see in her face what she knew she'd lost. That she knew she would never look at her the same way again.

She left Dougie alone.

Maya retreated to her room in the attic and headed straight to her workstation, placing the envelope on the table. She stood still for a moment, deep in thought. She opened the drawer and pulled out the old glass lightbulb. She scrutinized it with incredible curiosity. Maya wondered how something so elegant and small could be so perceivably dangerous. How was this tiny, fragile object reason enough to send humanity back into the Dark? How could she, Dougie, have justified such cruelty? After a moment, she gently placed the bulb back into the drawer.

Her eyes went back to the envelope. Cautiously, she opened it again and took out the letter and clue. After inspecting them both, she reached into the envelope again and pulled out one more sheet of paper. It was, as the letter described, something written in an unusual cipher. Images, numbers, and strange shapes made up the entirety of the writing. There was no possible way she could decode any of it without the proper key.

Maya laid down on her bed, exhausted. As she stared up at the ceiling, her mind was littered with uncomfortable thoughts that made her feel uneasy. She felt as though she were being punished for something she didn't do. Maya didn't know what was worse: that she was being entrusted with such a massive responsibility seemingly beyond her years, or that she had no way of knowing if it was true unless she embarked on the journey.

In a flash, she recalled snippets of stories shared by some of the village elders about the days before The Wave. Most of them were not unlike what Dougie had just described: population dwindling down everywhere, entire countries obliterated in mere minutes, and how we might have shared the same fate. Although none of the village elders believed The Wave was ever a good thing, they were at least grateful to have survived to talk about it all. Something that might not have been so had things turned out differently.

All these thoughts rushed through her head as she rested in place, silent and still.

6

Acceptance

An hour had passed since Maya left for her room. Dougie felt a bit better but still not quite as mobile. She could still stand up and move around, but she took her time a bit more than usual now. She got out of her bed, put on her robe, grabbed her cane, and carefully made her way to her study.

Upon entering, she jumped to see Maya inside, sitting at her desk. She was so surprised that she initially didn't notice the prepared backpack resting on the floor beside her. What she did notice right away were Maya's eyes, filled with incredible determination—the kind depicted in the heroes of her stories. A moment later, Maya stood and walked over to Dougie. She stopped directly in front of her, gently taking her hand and placing the key inside.

"I've already placed the clue back where I found it," she said. "I've memorized it. I have my bag packed, and I'm ready to go."

"Oh, wonderful, Maya," exclaimed Dougie.

"I didn't say I was going just yet. I need you to tell me something," Maya said, "and depending on your answer, I'm either heading out the door, or I'm unpacking my bag."

"Very well, my dear," replied Dougie.

"Why me?" she asked. "Of all the people in this village to trust with your terrible secret and this colossal task, why me? Why not any of the older and more experienced people in this village?"

Dougie hesitated. Maya could see her searching internally for what to say next, to push her that one step further, to make this journey.

"You must make a choice," she finally said.

Maya felt annoyed at Dougie. Of course, she had to make a choice, that's exactly what she was trying to do right now! As it turns out, the "choice" Dougie was referring to was something else entirely. She wasn't talking about the choice to stay or go; it was the one she would have to make when she arrived at the machine.

"When Clarke began his experiment," said Dougie, "he may have prevented humanity's destruction, but he did so at the cost of your own free will. He made a conscious decision to shape your future in the way he believed was best for you at that time. Now, my generation is close to its end, and yours is just beginning."

"Where humanity goes from here," Dougie continued, "is a choice that must be your own. The only way this decision can be made, my dear, is for you to see the world as it is with your own eyes. To experience and learn how and if humanity is worthy of Power once again. My generation's voice has already been heard, my dear. Now it is time for yours."

Maya was dumbfounded. She had assumed Dougie merely wanted to keep the old fire burning, as it were. Dougie presented her great-niece with an old saying: "Whoever fights monsters should see to it that in the process he does not become a monster."

Maya stared into her great-aunt's eyes and shook her head. "No more anecdotes. No more stories. Tell me honestly. Why me?"

The old woman stood before her, bemused and sad.

"Because, there is no one else on this Earth I can wholeheartedly trust more than you."

Maya could see the sincerity in Dougie's eyes. *I can't reconcile what you've done,* she thought to herself, *but I love you too much to deny your last wish, unbelievable as it is.* She placed her hand on Dougie's shoulder, and said the only thing that was left to say.

"I'll do it," she said softly.

Dougie stumbled forward to embrace her and held her tightly in her bony arms. Maya returned with a confused and hesitant embrace, uncertain of the best reaction to the present moment. Slowly, Dougie released her embrace.

"Wait," said Dougie as she stepped towards her library corner. She chose an old book from a high shelf, opened it, and withdrew a piece of old folded paper hidden within. She returned to Maya, presenting the paper to her.

"You will need this as well," she said.

Maya examined the paper. It was an old map of the Western United States, ranging from what appeared to be northern California up to southern Washington. It was faded and torn, but it was still legible, with enough detail for proper navigation. Maya had used many maps like this old one and found it fairly easy to read, despite its advanced age. She tucked the map into her jacket pocket. She stepped to her backpack, picked it up, and walked back to Dougie, looking her full in the face.

"Promise me this," she said. "Stay alive until I get back, for Charlie's sake. I don't want him alone while I'm gone. I'll leave him with Joseph, so you won't have to worry too much. Just keep him calm and occupied like you—like you always do."

"I give you my word, my dear, I shall do my best."

After an awkward and understanding look at each other, Maya was on her way out of the study.

"Auf Wiedersehen, my dear," said Dougie.

Maya stopped, confused at what she just heard.

"I'm sorry, what did you say?"

"It's German. It means, 'until I see you again'."

Maya stared at her great-aunt, uncertain of how to respond. After a moment, she responded with a reluctant but affirmative nod, and went straight to her room.

Once there, Maya inspected her backpack to make sure it was loaded with everything she needed: food, camping gear, bandages, an old multi-tool, and a few pieces of extra clothing. She had also gathered a few additional items: her bow and arrows, her favorite knife, a spare one hidden inside her boot, and an old Horner Special 20 Harmonica in the key of "D"; her favorite musical companion for any trip.

She was nearly out the door when she recalled the unique hidden-blade project that she was still working on. It wasn't ready for use just yet, but she had a feeling it would come in handy on her quest. She decided that she could work on it along the way. Hopefully, it would prove helpful and give her something to do in her downtime. She picked it up, placed it in her backpack, and zipped it tightly.

Now, she was finally ready for her long journey. There was only one more thing she had to do before she left, and she wasn't looking forward to it.

7

The Promise

Joseph was hard at work at his blacksmith's forge, mostly making horseshoes and tools for the farmers. He enjoyed his work as it kept him outside in the fresh air. Well, as fresh as it can be while working with the smell of molten metal and smoldering hot fires. Even so, it never bothered him. He was happy to apply his skills to the village. While he was working, Joseph kept a close eye on Charlie as he was playing soccer with some other children. Joseph loved the sound of their laughter. It was music to his ears. He often thought of himself as a child at heart and occasionally enjoyed goofing off with the kids, earning himself the nickname "Uncle Joey," an appropriate moniker for his guardian-like disposition.

Joseph was surprised to see Maya this morning, looking all set to leave again.

"Maya," he said, "you're heading back out already?"

"I need to talk to you about something," she said. "Do you have a minute?"

Joseph was initially concerned Dougie might have passed on in the night. After Maya reassured him to the contrary, she impressed upon him the need for his help. With that, Joseph put down his tools and gave Maya his undivided attention.

Maya hesitated. Then, in one breath:

"I have to go somewhere for a while. I can't say what it is or why I'm going, but I need you to trust me when I say that it's important. And all I can tell you is that I have to leave, and I don't know for sure when I'll be back."

Joseph was nonplussed. "But you are coming back, right?"

"Yes!"

"Okay. Okay, good."

"I need you to please just watch over Charlie while I'm gone. He doesn't need to stay here, he can still live with Dougie, but Charlie will need to be watched by someone who isn't…hindered."

Joseph rose from his seat and placed his hands on Maya's shoulders, assuring her that he would do his best to take care of Charlie in her absence. Maya smiled, feeling reassured of his sincerity, and thanking him profusely.

"One more thing," said Maya, "may I take one of your horses?"

"No problem. Give me a few minutes and I'll have one saddled up for you."

Maya was moved by Joseph's generosity.

"I assume you're going to talk to Charlie before you go" asked Joseph?

"Yeah… but I'm not looking forward to it."

Maya seemed uneven, and Joseph noticed.

"Hey, don't worry. You'll be back. I know you will. Charlie will be fine, I promise."

Joseph headed to the stables to ready one of the horses. Maya took a deep breath to calm her nerves.

"Charlie," called Maya, "come here for a moment!"

Charlie did as he was asked and headed towards Maya. She kneeled and opened her arms wide. Charlie hugged her so hard it almost knocked her over.

"Is Dougie okay?" asked Charlie.

"Dougie's just fine. She's resting right now."

"Are you going back to the creek? Can I come with you?"

Charlie was getting excited at the prospect of spending the day with his sister.

Sadly, Maya had to put those ideas to rest for now.

"No, Charlie. I have to tell you something."

Charlie's excitement quickly dissipated as he listened to his older sister.

"I have to go away for a while. There's something important I have to do."

"What is it?"

"I can't tell you, buddy. But I promise you that it's a big important thing for everyone, including you."

"Can't I come with you?"

"No, Charlie. I'm sorry, I have to go alone. But don't worry, Joseph will take good care of you while I'm away."

Charlie couldn't hold it back any longer. His eyes began to water.

"Are you going away like mom did?"

Shocked, she pulled Charlie in and held him as tight as she could, doing her best not to shed any tears herself.

"No, buddy. Not like mom."

"But what if you don't come back?"

Maya gently pushed Charlie away to look him right in the eyes.

"You listen to me now, Charlie. I promise you, I will come back. No matter what, I will always come back. Do you believe me?"

"I think so...yes."

Maya smiled while still fighting back the tears, as she brought him in for one last embrace

"You know," said Maya, "you make me so happy! Stay strong for me, Joseph, and Dougie, okay?"

"I will," replied Charlie softly.

"Good boy. Now, go on."

Slowly, hesitantly, Charlie went back to the soccer game. Maya watched as Charlie did his best to get back into the feel of the game.

Joseph stepped in from behind Maya, the reins of a readied horse in his hand.

"Don't worry," he said, "he'll be fine."

"Thank you again, Joseph."

The two of them shared a glance. Maya moved closer and gave him an impulsive kiss on the cheek. He looked surprised, but unoffended.

She then approached the horse carefully, holding out her hand for inspection.

"Hey there, Stärke," she said.

The horse sniffed Maya's hand and immediately recognized her, allowing Maya to rest her forehead against its own. After a few gentle pats, Maya hopped onto the saddle.

Resolute, Maya turned around and rode down the long dirt laneway towards the main road. Joseph watched her leave until she was out of sight.

Maya wiped away her tears, and pressed on.

8

Into The Wilds

Maya rode for about two miles without stopping, before she decided to consult the map. Despite its advanced age, it was still legible. She recalled the image of the first clue, the dragon statue, and the word written underneath, "Yreka." She scanned the map carefully until she found what she was looking for. North of her position was a little town called Yreka. According to the map, it was at least 90 miles north from her present location, a four-day trip on horse with regular stops. It would be the farthest that Maya had ever traveled outside of her home.

The first day was simple—a gorgeous trek through the hills, open fields, and woodlands of the California wilds. Occasionally, Maya would stumble upon a few abandoned houses. She knew better than to look inside any of them for food or supplies, mostly because she could hunt and gather for herself, but also because there was no way of knowing for sure if any building around you was really abandoned. Maya had learned from some of her fellow wandering friends, both young and old, that there's likely at least one settler inside any given building. And without knowing which ones were threatening, it was usually better to leave them be, and not knock and risk your own safety.

Sometimes, Maya would take a break from the wilderness and ride along the old highways. She could occasionally see the long lines of abandoned cars and trucks, rolled to the sides of the road decades earlier when they all stopped dead and refused to start again. Massive chunks of rusted metal and broken glass lined many of the intersections. For some, this sight might have been as ominous as a graveyard. For Maya, however, it was a curious find. She had heard stories of these things but never ridden in one, let alone driven one. She often enjoyed finding strange treasures within these things.

Before nighttime fell, Maya decided to spend the night in an abandoned delivery truck. The trailer was empty, save for a few broken crates and no signs of life. Maya tied Stärke to the side of the truck and closed the door behind her securing it shut. She made her bed and rested as best she could. She found it challenging to get to sleep, not because she wasn't comfortable, but because homesickness was beginning to set in.

The second and third days were a little better, as the initial shock had worn off. Maya diverged from the old highway and back into the wilds. She took a quick hunting break and bagged herself a few rabbits for dinner. She also took some time to work on her hidden blade weapon, hoping it would work as she intended.

That night, Maya made camp deep in the woods. She built a fire and set up her tiny tent shortly after skinning, gutting, and cooking her dinner for that evening.

She was halfway through her meal when she heard a noise, not far away. Twigs were breaking on the ground, the typical sound of footsteps in the woods. She stopped eating to listen. But, after a few seconds, the sound didn't repeat, so she went back to her supper. Soon, the noise came again, slightly startling Stärke. This time, she was sure someone, or something, was closing in on her. She quietly put down her food and drew her knife, holding it in a combat-ready position. She looked all around her, listening for the first sign of trouble.

Suddenly, just beyond the reach of her fire's light, the source of the noise appeared.

It was a fox. A female, and of average size. It looked like a typical wild fox: predominantly red-orange fur with a white chin and underbelly and dark brown legs, but there was one thing about this fox that stood out to Maya, even in the dim light of the fire. Its eyes were unusually expressive, almost familiar, and they were two different colors: one was brown, and the other was blue.

Maya kept her eyes on the visitor, uncertain of how to react. Stärke seemed to calm down a bit, now that the source of the noise had revealed itself.

Slowly, the fox moved closer to the fire. Maya made a quick gesture with her knife, signaling the fox to keep her distance. Surprisingly, the creature picked up on her signal and didn't advance any further. Even more surprising, she didn't instantly retreat. Instead, the red-furred creature sat down, just like a dog when so instructed.

Maya was baffled by this display. She had encountered wild animals before, but she had never seen any of them behave so, well, domesticated. She quickly tried to assess the situation. It wasn't going to hurt her; otherwise, it likely would have tried to attack her by now. She noticed the fox running its tongue along its mouth, a general sign of hunger.

Maya looked at the rabbit, still cooking on the spit, and decided to make a move. She rotated the knife in her hand, repositioning the blade.

"Don't worry," she said, "I'm not going to hurt you."

Carefully, she advanced towards the remains of the dressed rabbit. She gingerly lifted the still-warm entrails and tossed it in her visitor's direction. The bloodied meat landed about four feet in front of the fox.

For a moment she thought the fox would do nothing, and she felt undeniably foolish. The animal stood there, staring at the meat, as Maya stood by waiting for her to take the offering and run.

Carefully, almost delicately, the fox advanced towards the messy hunks of rabbit flesh. She sniffed it, inspected it, then finally, picked it up in her mouth. Holding the meat in her jaws, the fox looked back at Maya, who, feeling more assured of the situation, lowered her knife. The two of them shared a seemingly friendly glance until, finally, the fox retreated into the woods. Maya sheathed her knife and sat back down to enjoy the rest of her dinner. Not long after that, she went to bed.

Upon waking the next morning, Maya buried the ambers of her fire, packed up her gear, and moved on. *It's the fourth day*, she thought, *which means I'm likely going to reach my destination.*

After about an hour or so of riding, Maya decided to give Stärke a break from the saddle, and a much-deserved brushing session. She stopped close to a downed tree, removed the saddle, and brushed the horse's back. All the while humming a soothing tune

After a few minutes, Maya thought she heard a strange noise coming from behind her, that familiar sound of twigs breaking underneath someone's feet. She turned around to check, but saw nothing out of the ordinary. Cautiously, she continued brushing. But soon, she heard the noise again. She stopped, remaining calm and alert to her surroundings. She heard the sound again, only this time, it was getting closer, and fast.

Concerned, Maya stepped away from her horse and reached for her knife, only to be suddenly and violently knocked onto the ground from behind with tremendous force. The mysterious figure wrestling with her was human, evidenced by his aggressive human-sounding grunts and screams. Maya could only make out a tall, brown-colored blur, trying her best to regain her composure.

Fearing for his life, Stärke ran off into the woods at full gallop.

Maya guessed where her attacker's head likely was and quickly thrust her elbow in that direction, successfully striking him right in the face, loosening his grip on her backpack, sending him clumsily backwards. Maya tried to get back to her feet, but the shock of the sudden attack still hindered her. She stood up and drew her knife, as she intended, and turned around to face her attacker, only to be assaulted yet again head-on and forced to the ground.

Panicking, she managed to shove her knife directly into her attackers' leg, causing him to wail in pain. She then jammed her thumb into his eye, forcing the stranger to fall onto his back.

Quickly, Maya tried to retrieve her knife, only for the attacker to violently kick her in the chest with his other leg, knocking the wind out of her and forcing her back onto the ground.

They sat across from each other for a moment as Maya tried to catch her breath while the stranger regained his composure.

After a few seconds, the stranger tried to pull the knife out of his leg. Maya, finally breathing correctly again, saw what he was doing and quickly remembered her hidden blade. She had modified it and was confident it would finally work. She aimed her arm at the stranger and retracted her wrist, activating the mechanism— much to her disappointment, no blade shot out from her sleeve.

By then, the stranger had successfully withdrawn her knife. He lunged towards Maya. In a panic, she tried to retrieve her other blade from her boot, but he was too fast and had her lying on her back; the blade closing in on her throat. When the stranger was close enough, Maya reached for the fresh wound on his leg and dug her fingers deep inside, causing the stranger to yell in pain and instinctively withdraw the knife from her throat. Maya sat up and grabbed the man's jacket with her free hand, trying to push him away, only for a fist to smash her right across the head suddenly.

She fell back, head screaming and vision blurred.

"Bitch," screamed the stranger.

The stranger raised her knife high into the air, with the tip of the blade aiming straight for Maya's heart. There was no question in her mind: *he is going to kill me. He's actually going to—*

Suddenly, like a flash of lightning, the stranger was hit by a red blur from the side. It was the fox from the night before, digging her teeth deep into the stranger's neck, surprising him enough that he dropped the knife and scrabbled at her fur with clumsy hands. She snarled, clawing at his grizzled face, opening large gashes across his cheeks and nose.

Maya tried to focus her vision, to understand what was happening. *Impossible,* she thought blearily, then, *have to grab my knife before—*

The stranger remembered the blade at the same time she did, and turned in its direction. But just as quickly as she'd appeared, the clever fox leapt down his body and tangled in his feet. His steps were clumsy and addled as he fell. Maya's knife, laid in the under-brush pointed slightly upward. He hardly felt it enter his throat as he slammed heavily onto it.

He bled out in less than a minute, while the battered young woman and the red fox watched from the ground nearby.

Maya slowly regained her senses. As she sat up straight, the fox stayed by her side. She looked over and saw the lifeless body of her attacker. She turned back to face her rescuer, who remained still, wagging her tail like a happy dog.

"Thank you," said Maya.

Carefully, the fox nuzzled Maya's hand. Almost instinctively, Maya raised her hand and patted her rescuer's head. The red creature seemed to appreciate the sign of affection.

"You're a tough lady, aren't you?"

Suddenly, as if she'd realized she was late for something, the fox darted back into the woods. Maya left alone, suddenly a little upset, but this was the wild. Besides, it's not like animals will just stick around because they like you, as lovely as that would be.

But a moment later, the fox returned. To Maya's profound surprise, she placed her catch, a small rabbit clutched in her sharp teeth, before Maya, as if in offering. A sudden breeze rustled the greenery around them, and rendered the clever animal beautiful in shadow and light. Maya felt her heart ease a bit, and she smiled warmly.

"Inari," she said.

The fox—Inari—approached Maya again, looked deep in her eyes, and rested her head on Maya's lap. She, in turn, stroked Inari's back and delighted to hear the happy sounds emanating from the creature's soft body.

Maya felt better than she had in days. She had a new friend and companion. And she had hope that things would only get better from here.

9

Facing the Dragon

Maya spent the night resting and nursing her injuries. Inari remained close by, keeping a watchful eye out for predators. Maya was still pleasantly baffled by the fox's behavior. She felt fortunate to have made a friend so soon. After patching herself up she tried to call back her horse, Stärke, but with no luck. It seemed she would have to make the rest of the journey on foot. Not her first choice, but the only one she had. At least, for now.

After making dinner for them both, she crawled into her tent, preparing for bed. Maya invited Inari to sleep in the tent with her.

"It's all right," she said.

Inari hesitated at first, but after sniffing the tent, she carefully stepped inside. Maya closed the entrance and laid down for the night. Inari cuddled up close to her as if she were trying to keep Maya warm. Carefully, Maya rested her arm over Inari's body, gently holding her close, as she did with her plush toys as a child. They fell asleep quickly that night, comfortable in each other's warmth.

The next day, Maya awoke to the feel of Inari licking her face. She was still a bit sore from her attack, but she could move around relatively well. After a quick breakfast, Maya and Inari continued their journey. It may have taken her a bit longer than expected, but after five days, she would now find the dragon statue, and the next clue hidden within.

Inari stayed by Maya's side, occasionally breaking away to investigate a new smell or to scout ahead. Sometimes, she would lead Maya to something useful. While walking along the roadside, still lined with abandoned cars, Inari stopped at one of them and made some loud whining noises at the trunk. Maya tried to get her to stop and keep moving along, but Inari wouldn't have it. Finally, Maya decided to see what the fuss was about. *If it's a skeleton, I'm going to be very upset with you, Inari.*

The car itself was a silver color with black trim and dark rear windows. There was a large "H" on the front and back ends. Next to the "H" on the back was the word "ELEMENT."

She examined the trunk and tried to open it, but it was shut tight. Still, her now instigated curiosity was determined to know what was inside. She ran her hands over the sun-warmed metal and plastic, investigating every crack and crease, until—*yes!* She found a hidden handle and a loud pop indicated she had triggered the latch.

What was inside was something akin to miraculous. The storage hatch was loaded with canned foods, and a few jugs of drinking water.

"Well, this is too good to be true," said Maya.

With no time to spare, Maya packed up as many cans as she could realistically carry and filled up her canteen with the drinking water. She pried one can open for Inari, a little treat for making such a helpful find. Even after taking a decent amount, there was still a massive treasure trove of goods inside the trunk. Maya realized this would be useful for the return trip, or maybe as a bargaining chip for trade. She carefully closed the trunk, then took out her knife and carved a small triangle into the silver paint. She marked the location on her map as best she could. And with that, they moved on.

Another two hours before they finally reached their destination, the small town of Yreka. Much like the abandoned cars along the highway, the town itself was barren. Its buildings were broken and faded. Trees and other such vegetation had overtaken the human-built structures, their roots breaking through the pavement. Many of the old storefronts were boarded up and locked down. There was a term for places like this, though Maya never liked it: *ghost town.*

Maya and Inari made their way down the dusty streets towards what they assumed would be the center of town. From there, they would find a tall building to study the area from atop, and hopefully, find the dragon statue. Though, this task might have been easier said than done. None of the buildings in this old town were any higher than two or three stories. Still, it was worth a try.

After a quick scan of the area, Maya chose a building. It was one of the few that weren't boarded up, at least not *too* much. In one of the windows was a faded hand-written sign that read "No Power." Cautiously, the girl and the fox entered the building.

Inari ran ahead to scout the immediate area. She didn't seem to detect anything dangerous, making Maya feel a bit more secure about entering. After a moment, she heard Inari calling for her. She headed to where she could hear the fox's cries, turned the corner, and saw a flight of stairs heading upward.

"Good girl," she said.

The two of them advanced up the stairs to the third floor of the building. Once there, Maya searched for access to the roof. She crawled through a window, instructing Inari to wait for her in the room, which she did, despite sulking. Once outside, Maya made her way to the very top of the building. From there, she could see the whole town and at least five miles of the surrounding area. Maya pulled out a small retractable telescope, a birthday gift from years ago, and searched for the dragon statue. After a few minutes of searching, she found it, about a mile or so north along the main road. Carefully, she made her way back inside, reuniting with Inari, and the two of them headed back downstairs and outside.

A good twenty minutes or so later, they finally reached their ultimate destination. The sculpted-metal dragon, despite its incredible age, looked magical. The sketch drawing hardly did it justice. It stood at least six feet tall and ten feet long, built of rusty metal, colored tiles, and shards of glass. As its metal wings appeared to flap in the wind, it seemed it could spring to life at any moment. Maya felt chills.

She was so distracted admiring the artwork that she didn't notice Inari was already digging at the dragon's back leg. Suddenly, she remembered the clue she had memorized. She joined Inari on the ground and helped her dig, impressed at how well the clever fox seemed to detect that something was down there. *Her sense of smell must be incredible*, she thought to herself.

They found it almost immediately: a small metal box, wrapped in a thick plastic bag, and bound with what looked like old shoelaces. Maya eagerly unwrapped the box and opened it. Inside was a folded piece of paper. Carefully, she drew it out and unfolded it, revealing another typewritten letter from Dougie:

My dear Maya,

If you are reading this, then
you have proven yourself a true
survivor. I am proud of you for
making it this far. You should be
proud of yourself as well.

This next clue is a bit more
specific, so please be sure to
commit this all to memory
before you move on.

Your next destination is
further north, about forty miles
from where you stand now. It is
a small town called Ashland.
One of the few small cities still
alive and prospering. This place
has remained unshaped by the
loss of power and has adapted to
the new age.

When you reach Ashland,
you must go to the Elizabethan
Theater and seek out The
Master of Ceremonies, or the
MC.

Once you find this person, you must recite the following sequence verbatim.

You say:
"You know, The Bard thought Padua had a Harbor."

The MC replies:
"He also thought Ancient Rome had clocks."

You say:
"And that France had Lions."

The MC replies:
"And that Bohemia had a coastline."

You must perform this sequence EXACTLY as it is written here. Your very life will depend upon it. Once the sequence has been performed, the M.C. will guide you to your ultimate destination.

This code is only to be used once. It will fall upon you to establish a new code for the future. So be sure to burn this letter once you have memorized the sequence.

You have undoubtedly faced many challenges thus far. I believe in your ability to press on, Be brave, my dear.

Good luck,
Dougie

Maya sat and stared in disbelief, in frustration, and in sheer exhaustion. "Well," she finally said to Inari, "that complicates things just a bit." She wanted to cry. *Forty more miles on foot,* she thought. *She's sent me out here to die. She was so ashamed of herself that she didn't want to tell me anything in advance, and I'm completely unprepared and didn't bring enough supplies or food and my shoes will wear out soon and…and…*

And for a few brief moments, she let the tears fall. She still couldn't believe this of her great-aunt.

As she let it all out, Inari tried her best to console her friend by resting her head in her lap, purring like she had before. Maya, still feeling overwhelmed, gently held onto her friend as her tears trickled down her face.

That night, Maya made camp and recited the silly sequence to herself repeatedly, trying her best not to consult the paper. While she prided herself in possessing several talents and skills, memorization wasn't one of them. A simple drawing and a single word were one thing, but a whole sequence of words in a specific order—with a mysterious conversation partner who may not be alive any longer—was quite another thing entirely.

"Dammit, Professor," she said, more than once.

She paced around the fire, ranting about harbors and lions, carefully doing her best to commit the sequence to memory. Finally, she decided to call it a night and resume working on it in the morning. She folded the letter and placed it in one of her hidden jacket pockets. She and Inari crawled into their tent and went sullenly to sleep.

10

Fetch

The next morning, they awoke to the sounds of birds singing. After a quick breakfast from one of the cans they'd discovered, they packed up and hit the road once more, toward Ashland. Maya estimated the forty-mile journey would probably take them at least five days, maybe even a week, and that was if they were very lucky. There were countless potential obstacles ahead. She was already so far away from home, and every step brought her farther. But she had made a promise, and she intended to fulfill it. And with her new friend Inari by her side, she felt as ready as she could be.

The first two days after Yreka were uneventful: a few abandoned buildings here and some overgrown vegetation there, nothing that Maya hadn't already encountered. But the third day of the journey brought something rather unexpected. Maya and Inari found themselves outside of another small town, formerly known (according to her weathered map) as Hilt. The town was near the California-Oregon border, placing them halfway to their destination. Even more exciting, there was a reservoir about a quarter of a mile outside the main town. And since her water supply was dwindling, things were looking promising indeed.

Maya and Inari made their way towards the reservoir. It was in a flat area with a wide field of view, about three miles or so. Soon, the two of them were within sight of it, but instead of the large body of water they had expected, they found something else.

Adjacent to the reservoir was what could only be described as a massive wooden fort. It was likely built out of trees gathered from the surrounding area; its outer fence stood tall, maybe fifteen to twenty feet. Maya took out her telescope for a closer look. She could make out people, armed with what looked like spears, walking back and forth around the perimeter of the fort. Two guards stood on either side of the entrance. Given her position and distance, she could not see the inside very well, but she was confident there must be a settlement inside.

"All right," said Maya, "something tells me those people control the water here. Probably wouldn't take kindly to us just walking on over and taking it."

Inari made a little noise towards Maya as if to indicate that she was listening.

"Maybe we can approach them, offer a trade of some kind."

Maya sat down on the ground for a moment. Inari sat down right beside her.

"Okay, we'll just wait and watch for a little while. See if anyone else tries to knock on the door."

And so, they did. After a moment, Maya got up and thought about what to do in the meantime. Suddenly, she realized that there was something she hadn't tried yet. Maya looked at Inari and a curious thought went across her mind. Inari, in turn, looked up at Maya, apparently wondering what she was thinking.

Maya reached into her pack and pulled out a little ball. She always had one handy for Charlie or one of their dogs to play with when scavenging or hunting.

Inari seemed to recognize the little sphere in Maya's hand instantly, as if she had seen one before. She wagged her tail with extreme enthusiasm and leaned her upper body downward, with her front legs outstretched and her head down onto the ground, keeping her dual-colored eyes on the ball.

Maya was, once again, pleasantly surprised at Inari's dog-like behavior. She couldn't help but wonder if this was evolution…or something else. In any case, Maya was happy to play for a while and gleefully tossed the ball, prompting Inari to chase after it, retrieve it, and bring it right back to her. It seemed neither one of them could recall the last time they felt such joy.

After a few minutes, Maya looked over towards the fort again and noticed what looked like a small caravan approaching the front gate. Maya took the ball from Inari and placed it back into her backpack after quickly wiping it down, as she gave Inari a loving pat on the head.

"Good girl," she said, "that's enough for now."

Maya took out her telescope and carefully observed the situation. She could see at least four people approaching the gate: two on horseback, while the others drove a donkey-wagon, likely filled with trade goods. They stopped a few yards away from the gate as the guards readied their spears. One of the riders dismounted from his horse and took out what looked like a white rag from his pocket, holding it high into the air. He then said something to the guards, though Maya was too far away to hear it. After a moment, the gate opened, and a few more people came out to greet the new arrivals. One of them, a woman, embraced the man with the white rag as they escorted the caravan into the fort.

"Okay, I think that shows they're civil, to an extent. Let's hope they're not too wary of strangers."

11

The Trade Post

Maya and Inari approached the fort-village with incredible trepidation. Even as she held her white sock in her raised hands, and walked towards the gate as casually as possible, it was nerve-wracking. Those people she saw entering the village earlier could have been residents coming home from a supply run, or they could have been regular traders returning for business. Who knows how they might respond to a stranger? All these thoughts raced through Maya's head as she and the fox moved towards the guarded door of the strange fort.

Once they were within sight of the guards, they saw them ready their spears, taking a defensive stance. Maya noticed a sizable box-like thing next to the gate. All remained silent until she and Inari were five yards out.

"That's close enough," shouted one of the guards.

Maya stopped in her tracks. Inari followed her example and sat in place.

"State your business!"

Maya hesitated. Her nerves started to overtake her.

"I said state your business here!"

"Uh…my name is Maya Douglass, and—" she gestured to the fox "this is…my friend, Inari."

"Your business, Maya. Right now!"

"We were hoping to make a trade for some water."

The guards looked at each other for a moment. One of them nodded. Maya's heart started pounding as if trying to escape her chest. Inari sensed her friend's fears and did her best to calm her down, rubbing her face against her leg.

After what felt like an eternity, the first guard lowered her spear while her counterpart maintained his combat-ready stance. The female guard stepped a little closer to the girl and the fox.

"Do you have any weapons?" she asked, brusquely.

"I…I have a bow & arrows, and a knife on my belt. And one more in my boot," replied Maya.

"All right. I must ask that you hand them over to us. You'll get them all back when you're ready to leave."

Maya hesitated. She didn't like the idea of disarming in a completely new and strange environment, especially since she had no way of knowing if this guard would be faithful to her word. Maya looked at Inari, who looked back up at her with an expression that seemed to put her at ease. Maya's thinking was if Inari was calm, then she could be as well. *Animals tend to have a better sense of possible danger than most people,* she considered.

"All right," said Maya finally, "how do I…how do you want me to do it?"

"Step forward and place them on the ground. Then, take three paces back and wait a moment. I'll take care of it."

Maya did as she was asked. She carefully removed her bow and quiver of arrows, and both of her knives. She set them gently on the ground in front of her, and took a few large steps backward, followed by a scampering Inari. She watched as the guard stepped up to take her weapons and place them inside the mysterious box thing next to the gate. It was, she now understood, an old tool chest used for storage. The guard took a piece of paper, wrote down a number on the top and bottom, tore the paper in half, placed one piece inside the box with Maya's weapons, and presented the other half to Maya herself.

"All right," said the female guard, "when you get inside, go straight to the main office. You'll need to register with the village for future dealings. It's a big building with a giant "M" sign. You can't miss it. If you don't have any registration, they won't let you trade."

"Thank you."

The guard looked at her partner and gestured for him to lower his spear, which he reluctantly did. She approached the gate and banged on the door a few times. Not long after that, the gates opened, allowing Maya to enter.

She could not believe what she saw.

Inside the walls was a bustling village, with dozens of people moving in every direction. Voices were arguing and brokering deals with each other, negotiating trades and the value of goods. It was a massive citadel.

"Welcome to The Trade Post," said the guard as she gestured for Maya and Inari to walk through.

The massive gates boomed shut behind them as the two of them entered the city.

12

Kali

Although she was astonished by the bustle and life of this place, Maya understood the potential for real danger here. Even so, she was confident in her ability to defend herself should the occasion call for it. She remembered, a little late, that she'd forgotten to check her hidden blade with the guards outside the gate. Hopefully, she wouldn't have to use it. Assuming she managed to fix it well enough to actually work.

Maya and Inari made their way through the busy streets of The Trade Post. The air smelled of street-cooked meats and tanned leather, and rang with the sounds of the crowds of people talking over each other, discussing this, and debating that. Sometimes, Inari would become too fixated on some food seller and try to sneak in for a bite of something, only for Maya to catch her in the act before any damage could be done. She remembered how often she'd had to ensure Charlie was on his best behavior during special events and mealtimes, and felt heartsick missing him.

After several minutes of admiring the town, Maya finally saw her destination. It was a strange-shaped building with a sign close to it in the shape of a giant "M," as the guards had described it. Upon further examination, she also noticed what appeared to be a giant play structure for children—built out of colorful tubes, faded from prolonged exposure to the sun. Hearing the children's laughter as they played was bittersweet.

Maya and Inari walked inside the main building. It was loaded with old strange-looking furniture, filled with people waiting around or writing something down. Near the center of the room was a large counter. Behind it was a series of wooden signs with hand-painted writing on them. One sign read "Submit Completed Forms Here," and another read "Assistance." The center board read "Registration," so this was the one they approached.

They were greeted by a handsome young man with a cheery demeanor. "Hello there," he said, "I'm David. How can I help you?"

Maya hesitated, uncertain of how to respond. "I... I'm not sure."

"Is this your first time here at The Trade Post?"

"Yes."

"Are you looking to move in, start a business, or just make a single trade?"

After a quick discussion and answering a few more questions, Maya informed the young man of her desire to trade for some water, at least five days' worth. It was then that David noted they would have to bring this matter to the boss, as water is apparently their most expensive commodity. Maya was baffled by this and inquired how expensive it was.

"Please, follow me," said David. The young man turned to the area behind the counter. "Mike, I need you to watch the front for a while," he shouted towards the back.

A moment later, another man, apparently Mike, stepped out and took a spot at the registration counter. David walked around to the other side and met Maya and Inari. "This way, please," he said with a smile as he led them out the front door.

They walked rapidly down the narrow road, passing more bustling storefronts, until finally reaching their destination, an old fancy-looking house with an elegant front porch.

The young man held the door open for Maya but stopped her just before entering.

"I'm so sorry, but no pets are allowed inside the Boss's house."

Maya looked at Inari, who didn't seem to appreciate being referred to as a "pet." She was forming a tart reply when they were suddenly interrupted, by a voice emanating from inside the house.

"Oh, just let them in, David," said the voice. "There's no need to make a fuss."

The young man's confidence faded into nothingness. He suddenly seemed as if he were face-to-face with an iron-fisted king.

"Yes, very well, Boss. It's just that..."

"The house rules are my own, David. I can bend them as I please. You two. Please, come in."

"Yes. Understood, boss." David retreated like a frightened kitten.

Maya and Inari entered the house.

"Close the door behind you, won't you please?"

Maya did as she was asked, looked up, and saw the source of the voice. It was a woman, maybe in her mid-fifties. She was about as tall as Maya, if not just a bit taller, and appeared just as athletic. Her raven hair was long and hung over her shoulders like elegant drapes. Her dark green eyes twinkled in the light, accenting her surprisingly smooth face. It was with confidence and a sense of dominating power that she walked—a stark contrast to her incredibly polite demeanor, like a charming but scheming queen from a fairy tale. The house seemed ripped right out of the same cloth. Probably the only thing that seemed somewhat out of place was the old six-shooter strapped to her waist. Maya wondered if it still worked or if it was just for show. She wasn't about to test either theory.

Maya was slightly taken aback by this woman's strange presence. She was expecting a hardened, bitter creature based on David's reaction to her voice. Yet, it felt more like she was about to receive a plate of cookies.

"Welcome to The Trade Post," she said. "I'm Kali, the Mayor."

Inari seemed somewhat wary of Kali and displayed her uncertainty with a few quiet whimpers.

"It's all right, Inari," said Maya. "I'm sorry, she takes a while to warm up to other people."

"That's quite all right," responded Kali. "I understand."

"Thank you for seeing me. Although, I'm not sure why I couldn't just make my trade with David."

"You must have asked for water."

"Yes, I did."

"Well, let's have a seat, and I'll explain it to you."

Kali gestured to Maya to take a seat on the couch, politely requesting that she keep her red-furred friend off the furniture. As Maya sat on the couch, she gestured for Inari to lay down by her feet. She did, all the while keeping her eyes on their host.

Kali sat down in an elegant chair opposite the couch.

"You see," she began, "we trade all sorts of goods here in my little village. Small trades like supplies, pelts, and so on are easy to come across. I let those traders move around as they please. But water, on the other hand, is a precious commodity around here. We happen to have the largest supply of it for miles. We also pride ourselves in taking the necessary time to ensure it's safe to drink. Those who live here in our village always have plenty of water for themselves. We can't just sell it to any random trader. They have to earn our trust."

Maya wasn't sure about any of this, but there was no guarantee that she would find another suitable water source between here and Ashland. Also, it was too much of a risk considering the nature of her journey. Against her better instincts, she decided to play the game.

"All right," replied Maya. "So, what can I do to earn your trust enough to trade for your water?"

"If you want to take some of our water," said Kali, "we will require a substantial trade. Something that can provide incredible benefit to most, if not all, of the people in my village."

Maya thought about what she could trade for the water. She didn't have a lot of stuff on her, and she didn't want to give the exact location of her home village for any potential future trading. Even though these people seemed civilized, and Kali had been more than hospitable so far, there was still no reason to trust her or anyone else in this town. For a moment, Maya couldn't think of anything of enough value for the water that she knew she needed. Then, she remembered.

"How about a large cache of canned food along with some extra drinking water?"

Kali seemed intrigued; her eyes narrowed.

"Do you have that? What would you need, then, with our water here?"

Maya flushed, realizing at once how ridiculous she sounded. "It's not with me. There's a car on the old highway about a three-day hike from here. I can draw a map and a detailed description of the car. It has a recognizable shape on the back."

"How much of a cache are we talking about?"

"Enough to give some to everyone in your village, and still have plenty for later."

"That is very…substantial." She looked dubious. "I don't suppose you can prove this claim in any way."

Carefully, Maya reached into her backpack and pulled out one of the cans of food, placing it on the little table. Kali admired the can.

"I could only carry so much of it myself. But there's enough in that car for everyone."

Kali thought about this proposal for a moment.

"All right," she said, "here is what I propose. You and your friend stay here in my village while I send a small scouting party to find your little cache of food. If they find it, they will send a message straight back to me saying so. If what you're saying is true, then you can have all the water you can carry for your journey. If, however, I find that you've lied to me, and I've wasted precious human resources for nothing, then you will have to work for your water for as long as I see fit. So, do we have a deal?"

Maya thought carefully. She still needed the water, she was somewhat confident the food cache was still there—*oh please don't let anyone else have stumbled across it and raided it,* she thought—and she couldn't risk staying off the trail for too much longer. It was a risk, but given the situation, it seemed like a necessary one.

"All right," said Maya finally, "it's a deal."

Kali offered Maya her hand. After a brief hesitation, Maya carefully accepted and shook it. Kali's grip was firm and assertive. *Dominant.* There was no question that something was likely amiss in Maya's mind, though she couldn't figure out what just yet.

"I look forward to doing business with you," said Kali, smiling. "...Maybe."

Maya did her best not to cringe at the pain in her hand.

13

The Wait

Maya put together a detailed sketch and description of the car with all the hidden goods inside, along with an equally detailed map showing its estimated location. Once she had jotted down all the details, she presented the papers to Kali's hunting party: three tough-looking folks who appeared capable of taking care of themselves in any situation. Maya was reminded of the attackers she'd faced a few times while on the road. Inari didn't seem to care much for them, as evidenced by her quiet growling at their presence.

Each hunter had a caged bird with them. Most likely, their intended messenger birds. Kali greeted them at the gate.

"You report back to me the moment you confirm this girl's find," she said.

"Understood, ma'am," replied one of the hunters.

The gate opened, and out went the hunting party, birds and all. Now, all that was left to do was wait and hope.

Maya and Inari were presented with a decent room at the town's inn for their temporary stay. Kali had offered up one of her own rooms, but Maya politely declined. She preferred her privacy. Also, she didn't trust Kali or this town. Although there was little reason to suspect foul play at any moment, she and Inari kept their guard up.

As a gesture of good faith, Kali presented Maya with a small pouch. Inside was maybe fifty hand-made shiny coins with the words "Trade Post" stamped onto each one.

"These can be used for purchasing goods in the town," said Kali, "help yourself to whatever you may like. It's on me."

After settling in, Maya took the opportunity to work on her hidden blade. Inari kept a watchful eye on the door, ever alert to potential guests. Maya didn't want to consider the potential consequences of bringing a weapon into the town, so she worked as quietly as possible—easier said than done, when working on a spring-loaded mechanism intended to shoot a blade at least fifty feet per second.

As Maya tweaked and adjusted her project, she took pride in her progress. She finally managed to adjust the mechanism enough for the blade to extend and retract to and from her sleeve, making it a perfect emergency weapon in a pinch. However, it still wasn't quite fixed enough to fire at a threat, as Maya wanted. Perhaps she would figure out this puzzle later. For now, she took comfort in knowing it was at least at the ready for her when needed.

Feeling more assured of her and Inari's safety, she decided to venture out into the town some more. They took their time exploring the various shops and eateries. One vendor quickly became her favorite with their signature Mandarin-style beef sticks: bite-sized strips of marinated beef skewered on a tiny bamboo spear, easy to enjoy while wandering around. Even Inari grew a fondness for them, though she seemed to prefer the ones with chicken.

Kali soon invited them to step inside her house once again.

"Please, follow me," she said, "I have something to show you."

With caution, Maya and Inari followed her. They were led down a long hallway and into a pleasant surprise.

"Welcome to my favorite room in the house."

Maya was standing in the middle of the most extensive collection of books she had ever seen. Every wall was lined with shelves containing what must have been hundreds of books of all kinds. At least five times more than Dougie's library. Some of them appeared to have been hand bound with fresh leather. The smell of new paper was unmistakable. This wasn't a library; it was a warehouse of literature.

"Wow," she proclaimed.

Inari looked up at Maya, somewhat confused at why she seemed so excited but was comfortable knowing she at least felt at ease.

"This is my most prized collection," said Kali. "I spent the better part of a lifetime building it up. Many books around here were burned during the early days when we all needed kindling for fire. Some of them were even recreated right here in town."

"Wait," said Maya, "you have your own printing press?"

"Among other things," replied Kali with a smile. "You are welcome to enjoy any book that you wish, provided you are careful with them, of course."

"Thank you."

For a moment, Maya felt a little bit safer around Kali. She still didn't entirely trust her but felt less need to keep her guard up all the time. Inari didn't seem to share Maya's inclinations as she would still let out a quiet growl towards Kali if she got too close. Even so, Maya maintained close attention to the fox's signals, even when they didn't seem entirely appropriate for a situation. Whatever it was that made Inari so wary of Kali, Maya was content to play the part of the grateful guest, to keep things calm, at least for the moment.

Maya sat down in the comfortable oversized chair in the corner of the library, with one of the many books from the extensive shelves. Inari rested beside her, ears perked up, almost as if she wanted to hear the story. More likely, she was keeping her guard up. Maya found herself entranced by the smell of the old paper and the engaging story. It was the first time in a while that she felt comfortable and safe…however temporary it would be.

14

Dinner

Two days had passed since Kali's hunting party left to find the food cache. In that time, Maya had already gone through a small stack of books in the library. Occasionally, Inari would be struck with boredom and nag Maya for a bit of playtime. She was always happy to oblige, and the time passed without too much worry.

But on the third day, as they were heading out of the library to get themselves some dinner,

"Wait!" called Kali from behind.

Maya and Inari stopped just before reaching the front door, and turned to face their host. She was standing across the room close to the dining hall.

"Please," she said, "won't you join me for dinner tonight?"

Maya was a bit surprised that Kali had only now extended an invitation to join her for dinner. Still, she was interested in the prospect of enjoying a home-cooked meal over yet another round of barbecued street food.

"Sure," she replied, "I'd be delighted."

Inari let out a soft whimper, indicating her lack of enthusiasm for the idea.

"Be nice, Inari," said Maya.

"Oh, don't worry," said Kali to the fox, "there's something for you as well."

Kali gestured Maya to follow her, and the three fell into step as they walked towards the dining hall. As they turned the corner, Maya was astonished—an elegant room with bright walls lined with warm paintings, clean plates and glassware atop a small shiny wooden table. Candles illuminated the whole room with a warm and inviting glow. The smell of lemon and herbs dominated the pleasant atmosphere. It was like something out of one of the fairy tales Maya read as a child.

"Please, have a seat," said Kali.

Maya made her way to one side of the table and sat down. Inari was surprised to find a spot just for her on the floor beside Maya's chair. Kali took her place, and rang a little bell next to her plate. Immediately, a small team of servants entered the room carrying covered plates and rested them before Kali and Maya with grace. They even had a tiny dish for Inari. With a quick flick of their wrists, they removed the covers and clouds of pleasant-smelling steam escaped into the air.

In front of Maya was the most extravagant and delicious-looking meal she had ever seen. Steak cooked in what smelled like oranges and garlic, roasted potatoes layered with butter, and steaming white rice topped with cilantro and a dash of fragrant oil. Nothing ever smelled so tantalizing to Maya as this meal before her. Even Inari was presented with something unexpected.

Maya couldn't quite tell what it was, but if she had to guess, it looked like chicken stew.

"Bon appétit," said Kali.

"This looks amazing," replied Maya, "thank you."

Even Inari seemed to approve of the meal as she dove headfirst into the bowl of deliciousness before her.

Maya made a precise cut of the tender meat and took a slow bite. The texture, the juiciness, even the chewy bits from the char marks were mystifying. She could not remember the last time she felt so much pleasure from food.

"So," said Kali, "have you perfected your hidden blade yet?"

Maya's chewing stopped as she froze in place. Inari picked up on her sudden burst of fear as she sprang her head up, fully alert, ready for action. Maya briefly thought about trying to play dumb and pretend not to know what her host was talking about, but she could tell that Kali was too bright for that. She quickly scanned the immediate area with her eyes, looking for any signs of an ambush. As far as Maya could tell, none was forthcoming. She glanced down at Inari and noticed she was still relatively calm. If something were waiting around the corner, Inari would likely have noticed it by now. After taking a deep breath, Maya did the only thing she thought was right.

"How did you know?" she asked.

"My dear," replied Kali, "very few things happen in my town without me knowing about it. I suspected you were hiding something from the moment you set foot inside. But there was no need for me to be…impolite."

"Am I in danger?"

"Only if you're serious about using that thing on me."

"No. I mean not…I mean, well, I haven't had a reason to do so. Yet." She cringed inwardly.

Kali smiled. "Then, why don't we keep it that way?"

"Fine by me."

An uncomfortable silence fell upon the room. Maya was still on her guard after the initial shock. Her general thought was that if Inari didn't sense any potential danger, there likely wasn't any. At least, not yet.

"Listen, my dear," said Kali, "I've hosted a few travelers in my house before. In fact, one was from your home village down south."

"My…home village?"

"Indeed! Douglass Ranch, wasn't it?" Maya's heart was slowly turning to ice. "I'm willing to bet that you've at least heard of her."

"Her?"

"Her! Tell me, are you familiar with the name Mae Douglass?"

For a moment, Maya froze.

"I…" *what can I say?* "She's my great-aunt. I know her. Yes."

"Ah yes," said Kali, smiling. "I suspected you were related. When you gave your name at the gate, I was immediately reminded of her." She speared a bit of potato with the sharp tines of her fork. "She's been here a few times, you know. 'Off to visit old friends,' she always said. And yet, I always felt this air of mystery to her words. Like there was something else she was up to, but wouldn't say."

"Well. That does sound like her."

"Ah…you *do* know what I mean. Excellent." Kali's smile spread even wider, to show her teeth.

Maya felt terribly uneasy. Inari seemed to pick up on her feelings and stood up, ready to take on any danger that might be lurking around the corner. She was smart enough not to make any noise to avoid losing the upper hand, if in fact they had one. Maya wasn't sure.

She stayed in her seat, trying to appear calm. *What does she know*, Maya wondered? *What can she tell me?*

"So," said Maya, "it sounds like you two know each other pretty well."

"Oh, only a little. The Professor must have some wonderful friends up north if she's willing to make the hike so often. And always on foot!" She laughed, like bells tolling in a nighttime breeze. "Never on a horse or any wheels. As if in some strange penance. Like a monk." She turned her attention back to her guest. "Tell me, my dear, why didn't she come with you? I'm sure she wouldn't have wanted to miss seeing her friends."

Maya could sense there was something off about Kali's tone. Although she had no idea why Kali was so interested in Dougie, she could tell that, whatever it was, it likely wasn't good. She did her best to maintain her composure, despite her nerves hitting her hard. "She…she wanted to, but her health is starting to fade. She sent me to deliver a message to her friends, asking them to come down and be with her. She doesn't know how much longer she has."

For a moment, Kali seemed genuinely concerned by this.

"Oh my," she said, "I'm so sorry to hear that. How was she before you left?"

"She was…she was in good spirits, but she was still nervous. She's surrounded by family right now. Hopefully, she'll be all right when I return."

"Oh." Then, awkwardly, almost shyly, Kali said, "Thank you for telling me."

The tension seemed to lower a bit…only for it to suddenly rise again with a loud knocking at the front door.

Kali rose and answered it. It was the same young man that Maya encountered in the registration building when she first arrived…Daniel? David. He handed Kali a piece of paper folded neatly into a square. Then, as soon as he arrived, he left.

Kali immediately opened the letter and scanned the contents. A moment later, she returned to the dining table.

"Well," she said, "it would seem your story was true. My hunting party found your little stash of food and water. They are packing it up and heading back as we speak."

"That's great news!"

"Indeed. I shall have your water permit completed by tomorrow morning. In the meantime, let us finish our dinner together, shall we?"

They did, silent but slightly more relaxed in each other's company.

That night, Maya couldn't sleep well. She was still uncertain of her position. What if Kali or her minions barged into her room and locked her up? Not to mention, why was she so interested in Dougie? It made sense that she would likely have passed through this place a few times when she was making her regular trips to the machine, but there's no way that Kali was in on her secret. Unless there was something else going on that Maya hadn't thought of yet.

Despite her nerves getting the better of her, she managed to get some sleep, thanks to Inari's relentless watch of the area. Maya knew she could always feel safe when Inari was around. And the next day, she woke up, still in her room. Everything appeared to be safe and in order—even Inari was snoozing restfully. Maya carefully got out of bed and packed her bag. When she was ready, she woke up the fox, and they headed out.

The two of them had just walked out the door when,

"Ah, good morning, my dear."

Maya turned around and saw Kali before her with a sheet of paper, offering it to her.

"You will need this before you leave," she said, handing the paper to Maya. It was a written permit for all the water she could carry, plus however much more she may need upon future visits.

"You kept your end of the bargain; now I shall keep mine."

"Well…thank you so much for your hospitality and all your help."

"Won't you stay for breakfast?"

"Thank you, but I should get going."

Kali smiled that same strange, dangerous smile. "I understand, dear. Well, I hope you will come by again on your way home."

With that, Maya shook Kali's hand and headed out. She made her way to the water shop with the note. The workers there filled her canteen to the brim with the clearest water she had ever seen. They also provided her with another, newer canteen, with a larger capacity, together with a few extra smaller jugs for her pack. After thanking the workers for their help, she headed straight to the front gate.

Without any incident, she retrieved her weapons from the guards outside. She thanked them politely and was on the road again, with Inari by her side.

A moment later, Kali approached the gate and watched them walk away.

"Shall we follow her?" asked one of the guards.

"No," replied Kali, "not yet. Round up the boys. Have them ready to move within the hour."

"Yes, ma'am!"

Kali continued to watch Maya as she walked down the path with a mischievous smile. The kind only made by monsters before the kill. *This one,* she thought, *is mine.*

15

The Bard

After two more days of hiking, Maya and Inari finally reached Ashland. They spent most of their time hiking on old highway 5 only to deviate once they saw the signs pointing to their destination on highway 99. They hadn't truly felt they had arrived until they walked farther down the road and found an old rusty sign with silver letters that read "Ashland, Oregon." It was probably one of the most beautiful sights they had ever seen on their whole journey so far.

As they progressed farther down the road, Maya thought she heard music. As she and Inari got even closer, she swore that she could smell bread, freshly baked. *Sourdough,* she thought. Her favorite.

With incredible excitement, Maya and Inari rushed down the street towards that sweet-smelling aroma and lively music.

As they got closer, she could see the lights. Candles and little fires, some of them covered in colored glass fixtures, like bursts of dancing rainbows.

Finally, they got close enough to see the commotion. It was more wonderful than she could have imagined—it was a party! From the look of it, a costume party. Everyone was dressed in elegant and elaborate outfits, gorgeous fabrics with detailed designs, textured with beads and extravagant shapes. They were all wearing masks, too—dramatic, colorful, expressive masks! Maya remembered the story of Cinderella and a great ball. The illustrations from that book bore an uncanny resemblance to the extravaganza before her now. For a moment, Maya felt as though she had traveled through time.

Maya and Inari made their way through the crowd. The people seemed friendly and inviting. Almost familiar, although a few of them cast sidelong glances at the curious red fox following the young woman like an obedient companion animal. As fascinated as Maya was by their display, she couldn't decide if she should be cautious. She looked down at Inari, who seemed to be calm despite the organized chaos all about. Maya felt a bit more at ease as the two of them ventured further through the crowd and towards the center of town.

The streets were overflowing with people. The smell of wine, cheese, and flowers perfumed the air. The sounds of laughter and joyful cries echoed throughout.

Suddenly, an older man approached Maya in a friendly manner. He was perhaps in his late fifties. He had salt and pepper hair, was a bit on the heavy side, and he wore a jester's mask, complete with little bells on extended points and an exaggerated long nose.

"Excuse me, young lady," said the old man, "but you appear to require this."

Before the older man could venture any closer, Inari growled and bared her teeth. Picking up on this signal, the older man carefully remained in place.

"Easy there," said Maya as she patted Inari, calming her down.

Gently, the older man leaned down close to Inari's level and slowly offered his hand. She took a few sniffs with careful diligence before licking it, realizing the older man wasn't a threat. She wouldn't let him pet her, but she was comfortable enough to let him approach a little closer.

"You have a lovely companion there, young lady," said the old man. He presented Maya with an elegant-looking mask, much like the ones worn by the others. This mask was cream white with a silver diamond pattern running along the face. It even had a few encrusted jewels along some of the patterns. Also, short silver and white ribbons dangling along either side.

"That is lovely. Please, would you tell me what's going on here?"

"Oh, don't you know?"

"I…just arrived."

"It's The Bard's Birthday!"

"The Bard?"

"William Shakespeare! This town has a proud history of theater. Today is the day we celebrate and keep his memory alive."

"I see. Listen, I'm looking for The Elizabethan Theater. Can you point me in the right direction, please?"

The older man gave Maya directions to her destination with enthusiasm. "You're just in time," he said, "there's going to be a grand show tonight."

"Thank you for your help," replied Maya.

"Wait! Don't forget this." He offered the elegant mask to Maya with a grandfatherly wink. "Consider it a welcome gift."

Maya graciously took the mask and put it on. It was surprisingly comfortable and made her feel a bit more jovial for some reason. Maybe it was the crowd and the music, but wearing the mask made her feel like a different person, however slightly.

"Thank you," she said to the old man as she continued her way towards the theater.

Along the way, she stumbled upon the source of the music. It was a live band with players all dressed up and in masks. There was a guitar player, a violinist, a percussionist, a cellist, and a flute player. They played with such harmony and enthusiasm that it reminded Maya of the music she'd enjoyed as a child, with her mother. She thought about her little brother and the time she held him up on her shoulders as she danced at a party—another bittersweet reminder of the significance of her quest.

Maya moved on. She and Inari soon found The Elizabethan Theater. Before Maya entered, she took out the last letter from Dougie and recited the code exchange a few more times to herself, quietly. She was still horribly nervous at her ability to recite the code exactly.

"Jeez, this must be how theater actors feel all the time, eh?" joked Maya to Inari, who merely tilted her head as if signaling her confusion.

After a few more minutes, Maya finally felt as ready as she could. As instructed, she wandered towards a colorful lantern and surreptitiously stuck the letter into the flame, waiting for it to catch and watching it burn quickly into black dusty nothingness. Maya had debated keeping it until after meeting with the MC, but she felt it was already too dangerous to continue holding onto it. Even though she felt relatively safe here, she knew better than to take the risk.

She and Inari made their way to the front entrance of the stage. Before she could enter, she was politely stopped by a young man.

"Good evening, miss," he said, "may I see your ticket?"

For a moment, Maya was baffled. "I'm sorry, what?" she replied.

"You need a ticket for the show tonight."

"Uh…I'm afraid I don't have one, but I'm here to see the MC."

"Is he expecting you?"

"Well…I don't know."

"You're not from here, are you?" he asked.

"No, I'm from out of town. I do need to see the MC. It's important."

The young man thought to himself for a moment. "I'll tell you what. I'll accept an item trade as a ticket."

Maya thought about it for a moment.

"Oh, how about this?"

Maya pulled out her harmonica and presented it to the young man. He tested it and found the unusual sound rather delightful.

"This should suffice," he said, "please, go on in. Enjoy the show. I shall inform the MC that you're expecting to see him. You will have to wait until after the show."

"That's fine with me. Thank you so much."

With that, the young man gestured for Maya and Inari to enter the theater. Once inside, Maya was in total awe. The stage was gigantic! It must have been at least twice the size of the stage back home. Directly above the stage was a massive opening revealing the late afternoon sky. Torches illuminated every corner of the area. Patrons were sitting comfortably in neat rows on padded seats. People in uniforms—*uniforms!*—were helping lead patrons to their areas. A few of them were carrying trays of what looked like drinks and snacks. It was unlike anything Maya had ever seen in person before. Sure, she saw pictures and read about venues like this in some of her books back home, and Dougie often talked about events like this before, but to see it herself was another thing entirely. She was a part of the stories now.

Maya took a seat towards the back. Inari rested at her side, apparently not as interested in the show as Maya was. It didn't matter, though. She just hoped the MC would arrive soon while the code sequence was still reasonably fresh in her mind. A moment later, a few of the sharply dressed folks put out some of the torches around the auditorium, dramatically changing the atmosphere. Soon, only the stage had light. Then, a flurry of music as a small band played an introductory piece. As the music swelled up, there was a burst of fire, a triumphant note, then, almost magically, the master of ceremonies appeared on stage.

"Good evening, one and all. My name is Michael, and I shall be your MC for the evening."

He did not appear old, although it was hard to say how old he likely was. Mid-forties, maybe. He had a rugged face, accented by a full, trimmed beard. His dark skin complimented his black hair, which was divided into dreadlocks and flowed with every graceful move of his dancer's body. Maya could make out some blue color on the tips of each strand. His outfit was contemporary but appeared classical in style: a flowing white open-front shirt with a chocolate brown waistcoat and navy jeans accented by his brown boots. He carried himself with a performer's energy and charm, like a storybook character inviting eager children to come along and play. Maya was impressed with his charisma.

"Gather 'round, my friends," he said, "for today is The Bard's Birthday! Today, we celebrate the words and truth of the theater! Today, we remind ourselves of the humanity worth preserving!"

The crowd cheered with contagious enthusiasm. Maya maintained a watchful eye on her surroundings. Not out of boredom, but out of constant caution. She was still on a mission, and she couldn't let this fun performance distract her. No matter how incredible it was.

She continued to quietly recite the code phrases to herself as she waited and watched.

After a fantastic presentation of scenes from Shakespeare's plays, comedy skits, and a few stranger things she hadn't heard of before, the doorman who let her in approached her, and escorted the MC to Maya and Inari.

"This is the young woman who wanted to see you, Michael," he said.

"Thank you, Tom," replied Michael.

Maya removed her mask and offered her hand to Michael.

"Hello," she said, "I'm Maya." *Maya Douglass,* she almost said, but something stopped her.

Michael took her hand and shook it with gentle enthusiasm. It made her feel at ease with him a bit more. With that, Tom left the two of them together.

"Well, it's nice to meet you, young lady," said Michael, "what can I do for you?"

"I have something I need to say to you."

"Listen, if this is about that fight from last night, I already apologized to—"

"No. That's not it."

"All right, what is it, then?

Maya took a deep breath and tried to steady her nerves.

"You know, The Bard thought Padua had a harbor," she said, looking him right in the eyes.

Immediately, a surprised look of recognition brightened Michael's face. He hesitated before responding.

"He also thought Ancient Rome had clocks."

So far, so good. She took another deep breath, thought about her words carefully, then spoke again.

"And that France had lions."

Michael's shocked face turned into a smile.

"And that Bohemia had a coastline."

A strange silence struck them both. Inari looked up at the two of them, uncertain of how to react. Then, the silence was broken with a question.

"How's Dougie?" asked Michael.

"She's all right, "Maya responded, "She sent me on this…mission in her stead. She's not able to make the trip anymore."

"Then she must trust you a great deal." Michael nodded. "Any friend of Dougie is a friend of mine."

Suddenly, the MC noticed something rubbing against his leg. He looked down to find Inari nuzzling his boots, like a cat showing its affection.

"She likes you," said Maya in amazement.

Michael knelt and offered his hand to Inari for inspection. After a few careful sniffs, the fox approached Michael and licked his face. Michael responded with a few appreciative strokes on her head and back. After a moment, Michael stood back up to face Maya.

"You must be hungry," he said. "Come with me. Let's get you both some dinner."

16

A Little History

The three of them made their way to Michael's home, a small cozy house just outside of town. It was two stories tall, painted navy blue with white trim, and a bright red door. Inside was an air of organized chaos: books and papers stacked as high as the shelves themselves. The walls were covered in colorful posters and paintings of all kinds. Littered all through the house were various candles. Some contained within glass housings, and some stuck in place after they had melted. Yet, despite all the seemingly random placements of things, the place felt clean and warm.

"Would you like something to drink?" asked Michael, "You must have had a long journey."

"Yes, please."

Michael made his way to the kitchen to fetch some refreshments.

Just then, a small figure emerged from around the corner. Maya quickly reached for her knife as a reflex. A second later, she realized what the figure was. A little girl, no more than eight years old, was peeking around the corner to see what the commotion was. Maya moved her hand away from her knife and knelt to her level.

"Hello there," said Maya softly. The little girl didn't respond. "It's okay. My name is Maya. What's your name?"

She blinked shyly without responding to Maya's question. Inari, ever observant, picked up on the little girl's shyness and carefully approached her. She extended her paw towards the little girl as she lowered her head, making gentle whimpering sounds as if inviting the little girl to pet her. Cautiously, the little girl approached Inari. When she was close enough, she extended her little hand, palm up. Inari took a few sniffs of the girl's hand. Much to the little girl's delight, Inari started licking her tiny palm. The little girl slowly raised her hand and patted Inari on the head ever so gently. The fox's tail wagged with excitement.

"What's her name?" asked the little girl.

"Inari."

"Hi, Inari."

As the little girl scratched the fox's ears, Inari licked her face, causing her to smile and giggle. Maya smiled, too. A moment later, Michael returned with two steaming mugs of what smelled like fresh tea.

"I see you've met my daughter, Izzy."

"Well, I haven't yet. Inari has."

They exchanged a friendly laugh as Michael handed Maya her mug.

"Thank you," said Maya.

"No worries," replied Michael. "Please, come and sit a while."

Michael looked towards his daughter.

"Izzy, these two are going to stay with us tonight, okay?"

"Okay," replied Izzy.

"Maya and I are going to talk for a while. You can go and play outside."

"Can Inari come and play with me?"

Michael looked at Maya as if awaiting an answer.

"Why don't you ask her yourself?" replied Maya, "I'm sure she'd love to."

"You want to play with me, Inari?" asked Izzy.

Inari turned to look at Maya and stood by as if awaiting permission. With her simple nod of approval, the fox was delighted beyond measure. She and Izzy ran out the front door like a flash. Michael instructed Izzy to stay by the front windows where he could keep an eye on them. Izzy briefly acknowledged as she bolted onto the front yard followed by her new furry companion.

Maya was impressed with how easily Inari made a new friend. She had always suspected that Inari would only behave around her. This show of empathy and affection towards others, especially kids, made Maya excited to introduce Inari to her little brother when it was time to return home. Maya's heart sank a little. For all she knew, Inari might decide to leave her at some point, and the two of them might never cross paths again. A possibility she always suspected but never entertained. Whatever was in store for their future together, she nonetheless loved the sight of her companion making friends with a shy little stranger. It reminded her just how kind nature could be.

Maya followed Michael into the den. Inside was an oversized couch, with fluffy chairs on either side. In the center of the furniture was a dark wooden coffee table with metal legs. Maya took a seat on the couch and was surprised at how cozy it was. Michael sat down in the chair facing out the window, allowing him to watch Izzy.

"She's adorable, your daughter," said Maya.

"Yup. She's my world. Although, she takes after her mother more than me."

"Oh, and where is she?"

Michael was slightly taken aback by that question. He held onto his tea a little tighter.

"She's…gone."

Maya suddenly felt terrible, like she had just unintentionally insulted her host.

"I…I'm so sorry. I didn't mean to…"

"It's all right," replied Michael, "you couldn't have known."

Maya regretted asking about Izzy's mother. She knew all too well the pain of losing a parent. In a flash, her mind was plagued by uncomfortable memories, full of tears and screams. Just as quickly as they popped into her head, she shook them away. Maya needed to remain focused. She took a careful sip of the tea to help refresh her mind. It was warm and delicious with a whole body of flavors—Earl Grey with lemon and cinnamon.

"Thank you for the tea," she said.

"Don't mention it," replied Michael. "Now, I'm sure you have some questions."

"Yes, I do." *I have so many.* "How do you know Dougie?"

"She recruited me, much like she recruited you. She and I first met, oh, about fifteen years ago. She was on her way home when she ran into a gang of raiders. She survived, but took a few nasty blows. She made her way into town seeking help, which I provided."

"You're a doctor?"

"Nurse…once upon a time." He smiled kindly. "At least, I was studying to be, before I fell in love with Theater."

Michael went on about how he treated Dougie's wounds. As Dougie recovered under his supervision, they built a genuine friendship. Overtime, Dougie became more trusting of Michael, and felt that he would be invaluable to future journeys. So, she decided to entrust him with her secret. At least, to a degree.

"Then, you know why I'm here," asked Maya?

"Of course," replied Michael, "you're here to continue her research."

She froze, her tea halfway to her lips. "I—well I'm no scientist like Dougie, but I'll do my best."

"That's all anyone can do," Michael said warmly, nodding at her. "She's worked for so long to discover the truth behind what happened, to see if there's anything to be done. Her friends up north have relied on her knowledge for so long, I'm frankly surprised your whole settlement isn't up here so she could study it full-time."

To discover the truth about what happened. Her head was spinning. Dougie hadn't told this man that what happened was …her. This man considered Dougie a trusted friend. He'd memorized that ridiculous coded message. Because he thought Dougie was trying to bring the Power back. He didn't know the truth.

"I suppose…" she began, softly, "she loved her home. Her brother's house. My brother and I grew up there. We've been all right back at the Ranch. And it looks like you're all doing pretty well up here."

"Well, this place has always been a haven for people, even before The Wave." He grinned. She believed him. There was a magic to this place such that The Dark hardly seemed to have touched it.

Maya got up to look out the window and admire the view of Inari playing with little Izzy. They were running around playing catch, tug-of-war, and so on. The two of them having so much fun together reminded Maya of Charlie and his playfulness. In that moment, she was reminded of how much she missed her little brother, and how determined she was to return home.

"Do you have any children," asked Michael?

"No. But I have a little brother back home."

"Well, he's very fortunate to have someone like you to look after him."

If you only knew Maya thought to herself, as she continued to admire the view of Izzy & Inari.

After a moment, she returned her attention to Michael. Her gaze was steady, and her voice didn't falter.

"Okay, what's my next stop?" she asked.

Michael got up from the couch and moved to one of the many bookshelves lining the walls. He scanned through stacks of papers, books, and random trinkets, until he finally found what he was looking for: a small wooden box with a tiny padlock. Michael placed it on the coffee table, reached into his pocket, and pulled out a collection of keys. After finding the one he needed, he unlocked the box and opened it.

The first thing he pulled out was a folded typewritten letter, which he handed to Maya. She took it without flinching.

My dear Maya,

By now, you will have met my friend, Michael. He saved my life many years ago, and can be trusted. He is not completely aware of the nature of your travels, but he does understand its importance.

Now, you are near the end of your journey. Your ultimate destination is due north about three hundred miles. A place known as Portland. This was the base of operations for me and Dr. Clarke.

I have taken the liberty of providing you with a detailed map of the exact location. It is a secret laboratory hidden within the hills outside the city. I must warn you to be absolutely cautious when approaching this location. Be sure you are not followed or seen by anyone.

One more thing: ask Michael about the "surprise" he may

have for you. It will make the rest of your journey a bit easier and more fun. Be sure to take the time needed to learn how to handle it properly. You will understand when you see it.

Good luck,
Dougie

Maya was shaking. *Three hundred. Three hundred more miles.* After the miles and miles of hiking she and Inari had already covered for this journey, it seemed as though it would never end. She'd hoped this would be the final point of the trip and that she could complete her mission and head home.

I'm not quitting, she thought stubbornly as she willed the tears not to fall, and endeavored to slow the furious beating of her heart. *I'm going to see this through. I'm going to right this wrong.*

Michael brought out the map that was mentioned in the letter. As promised, it was incredibly detailed. It even had a specific route planned out for arriving at the location. It looked like the intended route involved staying off the old main highways—lots of back roads and shortcuts. Yet, even with all that, it would still take her and Inari practically forever to reach their destination. Her legs and back were stiff and sore already. She was beyond overwhelmed. As she calmly regained her composure, Maya remembered an important detail from the letter. *The surprise.*

"What's the 'surprise' Dougie was writing about?"

A genuine smile spread across Michael's face.

"I'll show you."

With the box in hand, Michael guided Maya out the front door. Inari and Izzy were still playing together in the front yard. The two of them made their way to a large shed just a few hundred feet from the house. Once there, Michael retrieved his ring of keys again and searched for the one he needed. After a minute, he found it and unlocked the shed. As the doors swung open, Maya was greeted by an unexpected sight.

Inside the shed was a small all-terrain vehicle. It was remarkably clean, almost new-looking. It had a black-and-blue frame, a sizable seat, and a large basket in the back, just big enough for Inari to sit inside comfortably. Along the side of the saddle was a single word, "BEAST," painted in light blue and styled like a bolt of lightning. It was the most unexpected sight Maya could never have anticipated. She only had one question to ask.

"You're kidding, right?" she said. "Nothing like this runs anymore!"

"You're right," replied Michael, "but this isn't like any of the others you've seen so far. This baby runs on pure kinetic energy."

An uncertain silence hung in the air.

"Seriously?" said Maya.

"Yeah," replied Michael, "100%. Have you ever heard of a flywheel?"

"Yes."

"Well, this is basically the same thing. Just before The Wave, they came out with a few models of these. No batteries, spark plugs, or starter. All you need to do is spin a little wheel on top for a minute, and the rest will follow. It's basically a highly advanced version of winding up a rubber band and letting it loose."

Michael retrieved a key from the box and handed it to Maya.

"So, you're also a mechanic?"

"No, but I know some people."

Maya admired the machine before her. She had always heard stories about them but never imagined she would see a functioning one up close. She could swear that it was built yesterday, with how well all the parts were preserved and cleaned.

"I'll give you the crash course for driving it in the morning," said Michael, "right now, I suggest we call it a day."

Maya agreed and placed the keys to the ATV in her pocket. Michael closed and locked the shed containing the sleek four-wheeled Beast. Maya was suddenly lost in her imagination as she thought about how much fun riding this new and unusual thing might be. Little did she know how much of a challenge lay ahead.

Maya, Inari, Michael, and Izzy had dinner together that night at a gorgeous wooden table. Their meal consisted of barbecued chicken and grilled vegetables, including carrots and asparagus topped with goat cheese, all grown in Michael's garden behind the house. The savory taste of it all reminded Maya of home, and of her mother's cooking. The meal was accompanied by laughter and smiles all through the night. For a moment, Maya felt as if she was home again.

After dinner, they all retired for the night. Michael set up the couch for Maya to sleep. The sizable fuzzy blanket felt warm and smooth to the touch. Michael also had a cozy doggie bed for Inari, which she seemed to appreciate.

Izzy gave Maya and Inari the biggest hugs she could muster. With that, Michael picked up Izzy and carried her to bed, wishing Maya and Inari a good night. Maya crawled under the blanket and rested on her side. Inari jumped onto the doggie bed, circled inside a few times, then curled up into a ball. Maya stroked Inari's back as she rested.

"Goodnight, my friend," she said.

Inari gave a soft whimper of delighted comfort. Soon after, they both fell asleep.

17

Taming the Beast

The following day, Maya awoke to the smell of eggs and bacon frying in butter, mingled with the aroma of fresh coffee. She also awoke to the blinding rays of sun through the house's front window, causing her to squint and hold her hand in front of her face.

"Morning, sunshine," called Michael.

Maya stood and shuffled towards the counter. Inari, somewhat surprisingly, was still asleep, bathing in the sunlight. As Maya sat on a stool beside the counter, Michael poured some coffee into a ceramic mug and presented it to her. She carefully picked it up and took a sip. It was dark and bitter and delicious.

"Sleep well?" asked Michael.

"Yes," replied Maya, "thank you. Where's Izzy?"

"She's still asleep. I guess our little ones tuckered themselves out playing so much."

The two of them shared a laugh. A moment later, Michael presented Maya with her breakfast: eggs over hard, perfectly cooked bacon, and a fruit bowl. Michael filled his own plate, and took a seat next to Maya.

"After breakfast, I'll give you a quick rundown on how to drive The Beast. I assume you've never ridden anything like it before?"

"Can't say that I have. I always wanted to try, though."

"Right. The most important thing is not to be afraid of it."

Maya was about to reply when she felt something soft rubbing against her leg. Inari was wide awake, nudging at her leg and giving her a meaningful puppy-eyed look.

"I think she smells your bacon," said Michael.

Maya lifted a piece of bacon from her plate and offered it to Inari with a smile. She didn't beg for any more than she was given—shortly after scarfing the tasty treat, she nudged her head against Maya's leg, only once, then retreated from the counter. "You're welcome," she said with pleasant surprise.

"That is one smart fox," Michael commented.

"Yeah. She's a strange one, but Inari's been a great companion so far. I hope she'll get to meet my little brother."

After breakfast, Maya got dressed, and Michael went to wake up Izzy. Once they were all ready for the day, they headed for the shed where The Beast was stored. Michael put on a helmet, and sat in the saddle.

"There's a field down the path, about a ten-minute walk. Izzy knows the way. I'll meet you there."

Maya acknowledged with an approving nod.

"You should step back a bit," said Michael.

As Maya and the others moved further away from The Beast, Michael began spinning the small wheel before the main control panel. As he did, The Beast awakened. It wasn't like the sound of any car engine Maya had heard stories about. Rather, it was a strange almost high-pitched hum, like a large Bicycle wheel spinning too fast. Loud enough to be noticed, but not so powerful to overwhelm anyone's hearing. Even so, the unusual sound of The Beast caused Inari to jump away in shock. Izzy, clearly used to it, comforted Inari the best she could.

"It's all right," she said, "it won't hurt you."

Carefully, Michael rode The Beast out of the shed. He stopped after moving forward a few yards to speak to Maya. He handed her the padlock to the shed.

"Lock it up before you head out! I'll see you in a little while."

Like a black and blue flash, Michael charged down the path towards his destination. Maya watched with a little more concern than she had before. Suddenly, she felt different about riding that thing herself. After a quick moment of reflection, Maya locked the shed and followed Izzy to the clearing where Michael would be waiting for them. Inari followed, however cautiously.

After a ten-minute hike, Maya and the others found themselves before a large clearing, with Michael waiting for them near the end of the path.

"Okay, you ready for your first lesson?" asked Michael.

Maya stood there uncertain of how to answer. Inari picked up on Maya's nerves and seemed reluctant to step any closer to The Beast.

"Look," said Michael, "I know this seems scary, but I promise, it's pretty easy once you get the hang of it."

Michael reached into the basket of The Beast and pulled out another helmet, offering it to Maya.

"Go ahead, try it on," he said.

Maya, with butterflies in her stomach, accepted the helmet and tried it on. Much to her surprise, it seemed to fit rather well. It wasn't enough to calm her nerves, but it did feel a bit reassuring somehow.

"Excellent," exclaimed Michael. "Now, hop on."

Ignoring the butterflies in her stomach, Maya hopped onto the seat. Inari stood close to Izzy, seemingly uncomfortable with Maya sitting atop the monstrosity before her. Michael explained the various functions of The Beast: the accelerator handle, the brake, the speedometer, and the energy gauge.

"This being your first ride, I want you to ease the accelerator gently. Take it slow, allow yourself to get a feel for its power. It will only go as fast as you want. Remember, you are always in control."

Maya took a deep breath, gently turned the accelerator, and woke up The Beast. The vibrations of the motor seemed even stronger now that she was directly on top of it. Maya felt her nerves getting the better of her almost at once, and she instinctively wanted to jump off. Before she could go through with her knee-jerk reaction, she took another deep breath and placed her hand on the accelerator, gently nudging it. With a sudden jerk, she was moving forward ever so slowly.

At first, Maya felt utterly shocked. She had never felt this kind of movement before. Yet, after a while, Maya started to get used to it and gradually picked up speed. After a few laps around the field, she started to enjoy herself. The sensation of riding The Beast was unlike anything else she had done before. Even more delightful, Inari could sense Maya's change in attitude and seemed to celebrate Maya's accomplishment with happy yelps and jumps. Michael and Izzy were also cheering her on, yelling out things like "You're doing great" and "look at you go." It was one of the most gratifying moments in Maya's life.

That is until she suddenly hit a large rock buried in the ground, causing her to come to a complete and sudden stop, catapulting herself off The Beast and into the mud.

Inari, Michael, and Izzy all raced towards Maya to see if she was all right. Once they reached her, they were all relieved to find that she was not badly hurt, just a little winded and maybe a bit embarrassed. After a quick inspection of The Beast, Michael determined that it was still in good working order. It seemed the modifications did their job. Maya hopped right back onto The Beast and continued to drive around the field, getting a better feel for handling it. After a few more laps, she invited Inari to join her on the ride. At first, Inari was reluctant even to step too close to the thing, let alone ride in the basket. But, after a few words of encouragement and sensing Maya's newly found confidence, Inari jumped into the basket and hunkered down as much as she could. Slowly, Maya drove around the field, allowing Inari to ease into the feeling of being a passenger on The Beast. After a while, the two of them were riding like they'd done it all their lives.

After about an hour of practice, Michael showed Maya a few more crucial things about The Beast: how to repair essential parts, how to adjust the settings for driving on different kinds of terrain, and, most importantly, how to fix a hole in the tire. While The Beast was equipped with one replacement tire, there was no guarantee that they could all be replaced if needed. The best Maya could do was plug the hole and ensure it stayed plugged. Fortunately, with the equipment and knowledge at her disposal, the chances of Maya needing to replace all the tires were slim.

Sometime later, the lessons were done. Michael had shown Maya everything she needed to know about driving and caring for The Beast. Even Inari felt less afraid of it. With her newly developed skill, they headed back to the house for a late lunch.

"You want to ride it back to the house?" asked Michael, "Izzy and I can walk, no problem."

"Thank you," replied Maya, "but I think I've done enough riding for today.

You guys go ahead. Inari and I will walk from here."

Michael picked up Izzy, placed her in the basket of The Beast, hopped into the saddle, and drove off towards the house. Maya watched as they drove down the path, delighted in her accomplishment. Once Michael was out of sight, Maya rested on her side, holding her butt.

"Oh, that hurts!"

18

Auf Wiedersehen

After resting in the dirt recovering from a literal pain in her ass, Maya picked herself up and headed down the path. She ended up taking her time, not wanting to aggravate the pain and stiffness any more than possible. Inari remained by her side, sensing that Maya was troubled but uncertain of how to help. Fortunately, it seemed that a good walk was just what she needed, as with each subsequent step, the pain dissipated however slightly. By the time she and Inari reached the house, she was walking normally.

"I must say, you seem to have recovered from your little flight rather well," joked Michael upon seeing her.

Maya shrugged. "Oh, it was nothing," she said, "I feel great! No issues here."

Michael could see right through Maya's façade. "As my mother used to say, 'look at me when you lie.'"

Maya felt a slight swell of embarrassment. "All right, it hurt a bit, but I'm fine now. I can handle it".

"I know you can." Michael escorted Maya and Inari back inside the house. After another night of engaging conversation and great food, they turned in for the night.

Early the following day, Maya and Inari were preparing for their drive up to Portland. After giving Izzy the biggest hug possible and letting her pet Inari one more time, the two of them hopped onto The Beast. She packed up her supplies and a few practical gifts from Michael: a small tool kit, a few old books, and some treats for Inari. She checked the systems to ensure all was well and prepared. Just before she started the engine, Michael stopped her.

"Hang on," he said, "there's one more thing I want to give you. Give me a minute."

Michael headed back inside the house as Maya, Inari, and Izzy waited patiently outside. A moment later, Michael returned outside with a metallic blue box, which he presented to Maya.

"You might need this," he said.

Maya took the box, opened it, and was not entirely sure about what she saw. Inside the box was a well-kept revolver, silver, with a four-inch barrel and a black rubber handle with finger grooves. Alongside the gun were some cleaning tools, two prepared quick reloaders, and a 50-count box of bullets. Maya carefully picked up the gun and opened the cylinder. Six bullets were already inside.

"I'm not sure if I can take this," she said, "I'm good with a knife, and you need it more than I do. To protect Izzy."

"Don't worry about us," replied Michael, "we'll be fine."

As Maya examined the weapon, Michael presented her with one last gift: a holster. After some hesitation, Maya graciously accepted the offerings and put them on. Maya and Inari were finally ready to continue their journey with her ride and her weapons at hand. Maya performed one last check on everything, including ensuring that Inari was as comfortable as possible. Then, she turned the wheel and woke up The Beast. They were ready to hit the road.

Just before Maya hit the accelerator, Izzy came up to her.

"Will we see you and Inari again?"

Without thinking, Maya smiled and said, "Yes. We'll come and visit again soon. I promise."

Izzy smiled.

"Besides," Maya continued, "I'll have to return The Beast on my way home."

"No, you won't," Michael responded, "it's all yours."

Maya seemed somewhat surprised.

"But," said Maya, "I thought…"

"Dougie's instructions were very specific," said Michael politely interrupting, "she wanted you to have The Beast. I just agreed to hold onto it until you arrived."

Suddenly, Maya was even more appreciative of Michael. Before she could ask how Michael and Izzy were going to travel to her home for their own future visit, Michael mentioned he had a few more kinetically powered vehicles at his disposal. They weren't the only ones out there with toys like The Beast.

And with that, Maya eased on the accelerator and rode off down the path, headed north. Michael and Izzy waved as she and Inari drove away.

"Good luck!" shouted Michael.

"We'll miss you!" exclaimed Izzy.

Maya waved back.

"Auf wiedersehen!" she said as she handled The Beast.

They continued to shout fond farewells until Maya and Inari were out of sight.

Izzy looked up at her father.

"Daddy," she said, "what does 'auf wiedersehen' mean?"

Michael bent down to her level.

"It's German, sweetie. It means, 'Until I see you again.'"

"That means she'll come back, right?"

Michael held his little girl close. "I hope so, baby. I hope so."

Maya and Inari rode through town on their way north. As they drove through the main road and nearly out of sight, a mysterious figure, clad in a heavy duster and a dark hat, with a live raven perched on his shoulder, watched them from afar. The stranger wrote something on a small piece of paper, rolled it up, and inserted it into a tiny tube affixed to the raven's leg.

With a quick swing of the man's arm, the black bird flew up into the sky and headed south, cawing all the way.

The raven flew over the wasteland with determined speed and diligence. After maybe an hour, it began its descent. It landed near what was formerly known as Emigrant Lake—the broken-down signs still bore its name. With grace and poise, the dark bird landed on the arm of a woman, clad in leather with a scarf covering her face. She was riding a motorcycle, modified with the same flywheel technology that powered Maya's ATV. Behind her, two members of the hunting party from The Trade Post, also rode modified motorcycles.

The woman removed the tiny note from the bird's leg and opened it. The note read:

"Portland. Will follow and await orders."

Kali removed the scarf from her face. She smiled as she looked down the road before her. She wrote a new note and inserted it into the tube.

The dark bird flapped its massive wings and flew up into the sky again, heading north.

"Here I come, little girl."

With that, she and the others rode north, sending up clouds of dust in their wake.

Kali's eyes seemed to burn in the twilight sky.

19

The Encounter

Once Maya got a feel for The Beast, it became her new favorite way to travel. For a moment, she felt as though she was granted a glimpse into what the world must have been like when everyone had their own set of wheels and could travel such tremendous distances in less than a few hours. Even Inari found some enjoyment in the speed and the wind in her face. On long stretches of straight road, she would stick her head out facing onward and let the breeze stroke her fur.

With the power of The Beast, their travel time was cut down exponentially. While their travel time from Ashland to Portland would have taken them a month at most on foot, The Beast could have them reaching their destination in about eight hours, provided they didn't stop. However, with Maya's curious nature and the need to occasionally stop for potential supplies (along with breaks to rest and stretch), their journey would likely take around five days, a week at most, by her estimation. With her confidence at its highest peak, Maya was sure of her journey's success. The only question is, what would she do when she came face-to-face with the machine?

Over the next few days, as Maya grew more familiar with The Beast and how well it could handle any given terrain, she became proficient enough to find creative ways around obstacles, saving tremendous amounts of time. Despite a few close calls, including nearly driving over a steep cliff, it seemed as if nothing could stand in their way.

After a long day of riding, Maya decided to make camp and call it a night. She found a perfectly secluded spot just off the minor road. As Maya turned into the pathway, she saw a dark wooden sign: crumbled down, half-covered in dirt and vines, with faded lettering on the front. Once she got closer to it, she could read the words on the sign, which read: "Welcome to Susan Creek Campgrounds. Please sign in at the host site".

Maya found the idea of there being designated places for camping, a rather novel one. She had gone camping all the time with her family and friends wherever they thought was best. People back then were told where they could camp? That seemed pretty silly.

After parking The Beast in a spot close to the lake, Maya dismounted, stretched her legs, and quickly surveyed the area. Much like the main roads she and Inari had traveled before, the place was filled with abandoned cars collecting dust and probably serving as a shelter for a few critters. Meanwhile, Inari jumped right out of the basket and bolted straight to the lake, where she jumped and splashed all around, seemingly having the time of her life. Maya was suddenly reminded of her little brother and how much he loved the water. It was a friendly and much-appreciated sight. But it pulled hard on her heartstrings.

Leaving Inari to her own devices, Maya checked her weapons and supplies and quickly swept the area. She was confident that she wouldn't find anyone there, but it always paid to check. After glancing through the abandoned cars, surveying the surrounding trees, and checking the one main building in the area, inside and out, Maya could find no signs of anyone else there. Confident in her situation, she built a fire and made dinner. Maya and Inari enjoyed their meal together by the fire. For some reason, eating by the fire reminded Maya of another camping trip she took with her parents, and Charlie. Maya mostly recalled the ghost stories she would tell that made her little brother's hairs stand on end. Maya thought about telling one to Inari, but didn't think she would appreciate it the same way. After filling their bellies with a nice warm meal, they took shelter inside the main building and called it a night.

The following morning, after a good breakfast, Maya continued to work on her hidden blade. She was determined to get it fully functional before hitting the road again. After an hour or so of tweaking and adjusting, she finally felt like it was ready, and eagerly headed outside to test it.

As Maya made her way to The Beast to retrieve some materials for a make-shift target, she noticed something that wasn't there before: footprints. They were not her own, as they were much more prominent and fresher. Someone was close to their camp.

Suddenly, a chill ran down her back. Were they being followed? Was someone watching them right now? Maya checked The Beast for missing parts or supplies; perhaps it was a thief in the night. The ATV was still fully intact and did not appear to have been burgled or damaged. Her supplies were all right where she'd left them the night before.

Maya searched the ground again, looking for more footprints and being more mindful of her own. As she further examined the area, she deduced that the stranger who left them must have been a tall man, based on the size and depth of the indent from his weight. There were unusual markings alongside the footprints, a kind of "swoosh" pattern, suggesting that the stranger was wearing a long overcoat or duster of some kind. As Maya followed the footsteps around her camp, she recreated the stranger's path, trying to determine what he was likely doing there in the first place. The footprints started from the main entrance of the camp area, went straight to The Beast, circled around, and stopped short of approaching the building where she and Inari were sleeping. The footprints then redirected straight into the nearby woods. Whoever this stranger was, he wasn't a thief, nor was he a maneater; otherwise, she would not be alive right now. *Someone is following us,* she thought. *And they don't want our food or supplies. Someone wants to know where we're going.*

Rather than follow the footprints back into the woods and risk walking into an ambush, Maya returned to The Beast, packed up her gear, and prepared to hit the road again. After one final check of their supplies, she and Inari climbed onto The Beast and were off. Maya thought about who was most likely following her and why as they drove down the back road. Her first thought was Michael, since nothing was stolen and neither she nor Inari was harmed. Maybe he had another ATV handy and decided to follow them for safety. He had mentioned the possibility of running into raiders before, so it wasn't too far out of the realm of possibility. Another thought was that it might be someone from The Trade Post working for Kali. She did seem to know more about Dougie than she had let on, even though she never outright said anything about either. *Whoever it is,* Maya thought, *they must be stopped. I can't risk them interfering.*

During the next hour's travel, Maya formulated a plan to identify and incapacitate her pursuer. It wasn't perfect and it was risky, but it needed to be done if her journey was to be successful. She waited until she arrived at an old residential area with plenty of houses. Not ideal hiding places, but they could provide her with adequate cover. And they did not encounter any other people. After a few minutes of winding through the old roads, Maya finally stopped her engine and leaped off The Beast to find cover, with Inari following right at her side. A few hundred yards away from The Beast, they found cover and took up a discrete watch. Maya withdrew her little telescope from her bag and observed The Beast from her vantage point.

Not long after, Maya was getting more and more frustrated at the lack of any action. For a moment, she thought that maybe she was merely overreacting. Perhaps the footprints she'd seen were not as fresh as she might have thought, and no one was following them. Perhaps the stress and uncertainty were finally getting to her head, and she saw things that weren't there. These contradictory thoughts began to cloud her mind, and she suddenly found it too difficult to remain still or control her thoughts.

Inari, picking up on Maya's feelings, did the only thing she knew was best for the situation: she nuzzled up against Maya's arm and rested her head on Maya's lap. Maya, in return, stroked the fox's loving head, taking comfort in her company. After a moment, she felt calm once again.

After Maya's mind had calmed down, there was a sudden noise. A kind of sound that could only have come from another motor like The Beast. Carefully, Maya aimed her glass at the place she parked. Sure enough, a stranger was indeed on their trail, and it was definitely not Michael! It was a tall stranger, with a large hat and a long overcoat that reached close to the ground, exactly like the kind of coat that would have made those weird patterns Maya saw earlier at her campsite. The stranger examined The Beast, perhaps trying to figure out which way Maya and Inari had gone. As the stranger scanned the area, Inari didn't like what she saw and made her disdain clear with an assertive growl. Maya lowered her spyglass and gently grabbed Inari's muzzle, whispering to her friend. "Shh!"

A moment later, Inari seemed to understand and remained quiet. Maya aimed her glass and observed the stranger searching around the area, trying to pick up their trail. Maya had to think quickly. She wanted to know who this man was working for, even though she had a pretty good idea. She hunkered down, put away her spyglass, and formulated a plan.

Meanwhile, the stranger kept circling a wide area from The Beast, trying to find their trails. Finally, after a moment, he thought he heard something coming from behind a broken-down car several yards away. The stranger drew his large hunting knife and carefully made his way closer. Once he reached the car, he raised his knife and rushed around to the other side, ready to kill. Except, when he turned the corner, nothing was there.

Then, right behind him, there was a distinct *click*.

"Drop the knife," said Maya from behind.

The stranger could tell that she meant business. He'd heard a hammer being pulled back on a gun. Although he might have tried to attack, banking on the gun not having any bullets, the sound of Inari's growl made him think twice. So, he did as he was instructed and placed his hunting knife on the ground.

"Hands in the air!"

Again, the stranger did as he was told.

"Turn around!"

He turned to face her.

Before Maya stood a tall man, probably in his early thirties, with long hair hanging outside his hat and an unkempt beard. His clothes, save for his rugged duster, were tattered and stained—*probably blood from previous victims*, Maya thought, *or animals he's taken down*. She kept her distance, for her safety but also because of the evil stench emanating from the stranger.

"Who are you?" asked Maya.

"No one of consequence," replied the stranger.

"Don't play with me, friend. I'm not in the mood."

The stranger gave a confident grin.

"Who sent you?" asked Maya, "Why are you following me?"

An awkward silence fell upon the scene for a moment.

"Look here, little girl. That gun of yours may be loaded, but you don't have the guts to take me on."

Without hesitation, Maya fired a single shot into the ground close to the strangers' feet. The bullet ricocheted off the ground, creating sparks and causing the stranger to jump back a bit.

"You're right," said Maya, "I have the bullets! You want to test my guts?"

At this point, the stranger was less prepared to make any kind of move on Maya. It was now time to cooperate.

"All right, take it easy, little girl. I'll talk".

"Good, and don't call me 'little girl'!"

The stranger kept his hands in the air, palms facing forward.

"I work for the mayor of The Trade Post. She's interested in where you're going. Says it has something to do with bringing the old world back."

The old world? He must have been referring to the days before The Wave. *The Power. He means The Power.*

"Why would she want that? The world seems fine as it is!" Internally, she cringed at this. *If only you knew, smelly stranger.*

"Oh, you don't believe that, now, do you?"

Maya gripped the revolver tighter, willing her hands to stop shaking.

"Kali told me a little about you," the stranger continued. "She saw it in your eyes. You're telling me that you're not the least bit curious about how the world was before the lights went out?"

Inari could sense Maya's unusual state but maintained her watchful eye on the stranger.

"Well, it doesn't matter anyway," said the stranger.

"Why not?" asked Maya.

"She knows where you're going. I sent her a message before I tailed you. She's probably not too far away from us right now."

Maya panicked as she looked into the strangers' eyes.

"You're lying!"

"Are you sure?"

Maya tried to read the situation, but the nerves had suddenly gotten to her. What if he was telling the truth? Would she still be able to complete her mission? She hadn't begun to work out her own internal struggle on fulfilling Dougie's last wish or correcting her greatest mistake, and what if …what if…

All these thoughts raced through her head, causing her to lower her weapon slowly and unconsciously. The stranger caught sight of it and, like a flash, grabbed his hat and threw it right into Maya's face, temporarily blinding her.

Inari instantly jumped into action and lunged at the stranger, ready to take out a massive bite. But the stranger was too quick and, before her teeth could even reach the stranger's neck, Inari was struck down with a heavy blow to the head from his fist. The fox fell to the ground and yelped in pain from the sudden blow.

Maya quickly grabbed hold of the large hat in her face and threw it away. Before she could see what was happening, the man was directly in front of her. The two wrestled to control the gun, punching and kneeing each other and rolling all over the ground. Finally, the stranger head-butted Maya directly in the face, forcing her to lose control and drop the gun. As blood dripped from Maya's nose, she looked over and saw Inari lying on her side. She couldn't tell if she was still breathing.

"Inari," she cried out.

The stranger picked up the gun as he stood up and towered over Maya, and kicked her in the chest, nearly knocking the wind out of her. He made his way over to Inari, who, as it turns out, was still alive but apparently in shock. The stranger looked over at Maya with a grin.

"I suppose I should put her out of her misery," he said.

Slowly, the stranger aimed the gun right at Inari's head, pulled back the hammer, and placed his finger on the trigger. Inari could do nothing but look up at the ugly sight before her.

Suddenly, a whiz of springs and a small burst of air swooshed close to the stranger's neck. At first, his reaction was minor. He thought it was just a quick gust of wind brushing against his skin. Then, he suddenly noticed something unusual; a trail of blood running down his arm and onto the gun in his hand. It was so shocking and so unexpected that he dropped the gun. It was only fortunate for Inari and Maya that the barrel was facing away from them both before going off from the drop.

The stranger raised his bloody hand to feel his neck. There was a small blade embedded right through his jugular. How? He looked back towards where he left Maya on the ground. Her arm was extended and aiming right for his neck. It was the spring-loaded hidden blade that Maya had been fixing. *It finally worked.*

Before the stranger could think to try and do anything, his massive loss of blood rendered him immovable. The stranger could do nothing but collapse on the spot as he desperately gasped for breath. Within seconds, the stranger was no more.

Maya, bleeding from the nose and frustrated at the pain in her chest, got up to check on Inari. She was alive, still breathing, but hurt. She felt all around for signs of broken bones or signs of bleeding.

Fortunately, there were none, though she was also concerned about potential internal bleeding, but had no means of detecting or treating it if any was active. She stroked Inari's head to comfort her as she carefully picked her up and carried her to The Beast.

"We have to get out of here."

Maya gently placed Inari on the ground, took off her jacket, rolled it up into a makeshift mattress, placed it inside the basket, and carefully rested Inari inside. She retrieved one of her small blankets from her pack and wrapped it around Inari's body.

"Stay with me, girl!"

Maya recovered her revolver and the blade from the now-dead stranger, reloaded the cylinder, mounted The Beast, turned the flywheel, and headed north with the speed of a mustang.

20

Arrival

For Inari's sake Maya did her best to maintain a smooth ride along the back roads. Under different circumstances, she would have set camp and waited for her to recover. But with Kali presumably on their tail, Maya couldn't afford to make too many stops. All she could do was keep a fast but smooth ride to Portland and hope that her companion would be all right. Occasionally, Maya would pull off to the side of the road and check to make sure Inari was still breathing. She may have been a tough girl, but that fierce blow to the head was hard.

"Please! Just hang in there, girl," she said.

Maya couldn't stand the idea of losing her fox companion. The thought of death lingering over anyone she cared about was too unbearable. In a flash of thought, she remembered the day her mother died.

According to Ramona, the village doctor, she'd died of kidney failure. With no way to treat it, all she could do was keep her mother as comfortable as possible while keeping her little brother away. It was going to be hard enough helping him deal with the loss of their mother; he didn't deserve to see her at the worst of her illness as well.

It had been a gruesome number of weeks; managing pain, helping with meals (both feeding and clean-up), and assisting her to the bathroom. The doctor tried her best to ease her mother's suffering, but her condition was too severe. Maya was both relieved and brokenhearted when she finally died. Then came the task of consoling her little brother. The most upsetting and demanding time of her life. Maya was sick with her own sadness, and worse for having to care for her despondent little brother.

After another two hours of driving, Maya finally saw a sign that she was close to her journey's end. She found herself speeding towards a welcoming sign on the road which read, "Welcome to Portland."

"Look, Inari," said Maya with giddy excitement, "we made it!"

Maya drove past the sign, and made her way into the seemingly empty city. If people were still living here, they were not making their presence well known. Vegetation had grown all over the buildings. Trees that survived had overgrown their planters, their roots pushing through the concrete—old cars on the side of the road, where someone had pushed them after they had just stopped working all those years ago. Signs in many of the shop windows all reading some variant of "NO POWER."

After a quick drive through the city's outskirts, Maya found what appeared to be an old general store. She parked The Beast just outside, and checked to see if the front door would still open. Much to her satisfaction, it did. She quickly peeked inside for signs of life, only to find none…at least at first. She carefully picked up Inari, still wrapped up in the blanket, and carried her into the shop.

Once inside, Maya found an open space near the corner of the main room. She gently placed Inari on the ground and examined her condition. Inari's muzzle appeared to be a bit swollen but not broken, thank goodness. Maya took out some water from her pack and offered Inari a drink. At first, she wouldn't take the water for some reason.

"Come on, girl," said Maya.

A moment later, she finally took a few sips. Maya hoped this was a sign that she was recovering. She felt all along Inari's back, looking for any signs of broken bones. There were none. As Maya stroked Inari's head to comfort her friend, the fox gently licked her other hand. A moment later, she tried to stand up to walk, but Maya gently set her back down.

"Not yet," she said, "just take it easy for now."

Maya stood up and carefully searched around the shop. She filled a small bowl she found with some canned food from her pack.

When she was sure of Inari's comfort and safety, Maya sat down close to her friend and pulled out her maps. She examined them closely, trying to determine where she was and where she needed to go from here. Her destination was in the hills outside the city, close to an area called Arlington Heights. Her present location was somewhere around the old Portland State University, which placed her at an hour's walk from her destination. She was so close.

Even though she was ready to head over, Maya could tell that Inari wasn't, and it didn't seem right to leave her alone. Also, there was no way of telling how well she might recover. Not helping matters was the impending arrival of Kali.

So, Maya decided to do the only thing that made sense to her: she waited, and kept her friend company as she rested. The only question was, how soon would she be ready to move on her own again?

21

Stay

Despite having an entire bowl of water and food at her disposal, the fox hadn't touched any of it. She just lay there, curled up into a ball. At first, Maya didn't think much of it. They were in a strange place, so maybe Inari just felt a bit uncomfortable with the sudden change in scenery. However, they had been on the road for most of the day before arriving here, and Inari never skipped an opportunity for food and water after a day of traveling. It was unusual for the fox to ignore meals.

Inari was still recovering from the shock of that massive blow from the stranger they had encountered. Maya checked again for general signs of injury and found nothing. Physically, aside from the location of the punch, Inari was all right. Suddenly, Maya had a thought. *Could Inari be suffering from emotional trauma?* Animals had feelings, albeit not as complex as humans, but they did have them, nonetheless. What if that sudden blow from the stranger did something other than knocking her down? Was it a sense of shame, or fear, or powerlessness? Maya wanted to figure it out quickly, lest she run the risk of being spotted by Kali before reaching her destination, or worse, losing her friend.

At first, Maya thought she might try to cheer Inari up. She reached into her bag and pulled out the same ball they played fetch with before. Maya bounced the ball off the floor a few times, trying to get Inari's attention, but she didn't seem interested. Even after tossing the ball across the room, she saw her friend remain motionless.

Finally, after a moment, Maya leaned in and placed her ear against Inari's body. She could still hear her heartbeat, but much to her concern, it sounded as if it was slowing down.

Petrified, Maya tried to think of what to do next. But what could she do? Whatever was ailing Inari, she had no idea how to treat it. So, Maya just knelt there, before her friend, and watched for a moment. She rested her head into her hands, and stroked the fox's red fur ever so gently, all the while resisting the urge to cry, for fear of accepting what was likely coming.

"Please," she whispered, "don't leave me!"

Inari let out a quiet whine.

"I don't want to lose you, too. I don't know what's going through your head right now, but if you can understand me, then please, stay!" Maya could no longer hold back her fearful tears.

"You should see my home. There are lots of people there, good, and friendly people. And kids! Like my little brother, Charlie. You would love him! He's playful, silly, and so brave. Just like you! I promised my mother I would take care of him, and I don't think I'm doing a good job."

Inari's breathing seemed to slow down, becoming shallower.

"Inari, you're my best friend! I love you! Please don't leave me! Not now!"

Emotionally drained and physically exhausted, Maya suddenly drifted to sleep, still holding onto Inari for dear life.

As she slept, she dreamed of being back home with her little brother, and her mother, who looked as radiant as ever. They were having a picnic under a great tree by the lake. Using some rope and a nearby log, Maya built a swing. Charlie laughed and smiled as Maya pushed him on the swing, causing him to fly. With every swing, he felt like a bird. Maya's mother revealed her famous chocolate fudge to everyone, much to their delight. As the day faded, so did everyone's energy. Maya's mother rested against the tree, with her daughter's head nestled on her lap, stroking her hair ever so gently. All the while, Maya beamed a joyful smile.

With a bright flash, the dream ended.

Maya awoke from her place on the floor. At first, everything was still unclear from her fogginess. As her eyes adjusted, she was greeted with a sight more joyful than anything else she could have imagined. Inari stood in front of her, wagging her tail and holding the ball in her jaws.

The fox placed the ball in front of her, waiting for her to throw it. Eagerly, Maya grabbed the ball and tossed it down the long hallway. Inari ran after the ball, caught it, and brought it right back like a flash of red lightning. Before Maya picked up the ball again, she instantly wrapped her arms around Inari and cried. This time, they were tears of happiness and relief. Her best friend was here to stay, and it would take more than some punk with an oversized fist to take her down!

Maya and Inari played a few more rounds of fetch together, feeling closer to each other than ever before. After they had exhausted themselves with so much play, they were finally ready to call it a night. Maya went back outside to hide The Beast the best she could. Her first thought was to cover it with nearby tree branches, but that might be too obvious. As she scouted the area, she saw something she hadn't noticed before. On the other side of the building was a sizable metal door that appeared to roll up and down. Carefully, Maya tried it, and much to her surprise, it opened. She rolled

The Beast inside and closed the gate again. Afterward, she unpacked her sleeping bag and travel mat and placed them in the corner beside Inari's little bed. After one more check around the area, Maya and Inari finally went to sleep.

It was the deepest and most restful sleep they'd had throughout the journey.

22

The Hills Have Eyes

The following day, Maya awoke feeling more rested than ever before. She noticed Inari in her little corner, still asleep. At first, Maya was nervous that Inari might have still succumbed to her trauma, but was relieved to see her wake up mere seconds later. Before she could muster a sigh of relief, she was pounced upon by her friend with affectionate nuzzles and licks all over her face. Maya was undoubtedly awake now.

They ate quickly, and Maya packed and prepared to face the outside world. First, she carefully peeked out the boarded windows for any signs of activity. So far, nothing. Feeling assured of their present surroundings, Maya prepared for what was likely—she hoped—the final step of her journey. She decided to leave The Beast parked inside the old store, as it proved a good hiding place. Also, given the terrain to her destination, there was no guarantee that

Maya could quickly drive up there, so it was deemed best to proceed on foot. After packing up everything she needed, including her hidden blade and her holstered revolver, Maya and Inari stepped out of their hiding place and into the unknown wilds of Portland.

There was a general sense of abandonment in what must have been, at one time, a prosperous city. It was the first time Maya had seen such a great sight of the old world. It made her curiosity about the Days of Power even more potent.

According to the map, their best course of action was to avoid the highways and take as many side roads and hiking paths as possible. It might take them a bit longer, but it was likely safer being more covert. If she was lucky, Maya would not have to worry about Kali at all. Even so, she kept her guard up, as did Inari.

Soon, after passing through a thicket of trees, they made their way out of the city center and into a residential zone. Walking past the empty houses felt different from wandering the city streets. Every few moments, she thought she could hear the people who once lived there. Maybe it was the density of the trees and the houses, or just the general paranoia that can accumulate from constantly looking for potential danger. Still, it was a bit more unnerving here. The only reassurance she had that they weren't being followed, at least not yet, was Inari's calm demeanor as they continued their route. If Inari didn't sense anything was wrong, then nothing could be wrong.

Maya couldn't help but wonder what the place might have been like before The Wave. The proximity of the houses and the general pleasant aesthetics of the surroundings, less the signs of previous chaos, were all so…welcoming. At one point, she came across a tire swing hanging from a nearby tree and was reminded of the swing she made for her little brother. The same one she dreamed about just the other night. This place might have been like her home village at one point in time.

Soon enough, Maya and Inari found themselves face to face with an uphill road, leading towards their final destination.

"Well," said Maya, "things can only go uphill from here…literally! You up for this?"

Maya looked at her friend, who responded with an excited cry.

"I'll take that as a yes."

They ventured into the hills.

As they hiked up the pathway through the old neighborhoods, Maya was once again fascinated with the strange houses that lined the old streets. Up here, they were so unique and different from any of the other houses she and Inari passed by. Some were unusual colors like purple, and some looked as if they were built out of stone. It was like strolling through one of her childhood storybooks, a fairytale experience in every way.

After admiring the now-ancient structures, Maya consulted the newer of her maps. According to the instructions, she needed to make her way to a specific house at the very top of the hill. The house depicted in the drawing was on par with some of the houses she had already noticed in the area: a large one-story building seemingly built out of clay, as it resembled a group of ancient huts fused into a single unit with a central hub. It was painted bright orange and had oddly shaped windows in unusual parts of the walls.

Maya was to seek the next clue that would lead her to Dr. Clarke's secret laboratory, inside the house itself. The clue was hidden within one of the kitchen walls.

Having memorized the house's general layout and the location of the next clue, Maya placed the map back inside her bag. Suddenly, she thought she heard what sounded like a snapping twig nearby. Maya whirled around but saw nothing. She looked down at Inari, who appeared calm and unconcerned. Maya brushed it off as just random noises, and pressed on.

The house was probably a thirty-minute hike from their location, nothing the two of them couldn't handle. As they made their way along the hill, Maya heard another unusual sound from behind her. She turned to look but, again, saw nothing. This time, however, Inari did notice something, and she didn't like it. Her subtle growling made that abundantly clear.

Carefully, Maya made her way inside a nearby house and instructed Inari to follow her. Luckily, there was a broken window just big enough for the two of them to climb through. They navigated through the abandoned residence, making their way up a flight of stairs to the second floor. Maya chose a room, likely the old master bedroom, and shut the door behind them. She found a small wooden chair and wedged up under the doorknob. Quietly, she stepped away from the door, her hand hovering over her revolver, ready to draw and fire.

She listened for any possible signs of people following her inside. After a moment, there didn't appear to be anything. Maya was just about to brush the whole thing off as a bad case of paranoia when,

"What do you mean you don't know which house?"

A faint voice from outside the door was coming from downstairs. Inari growled at the noise.

"Quiet," whispered Maya.

Inari silenced herself.

Then, a realization hit Maya's mind. *I should have done this earlier.*

As quietly as possible, Maya took out the detailed map of the house and the next clue's location. She knew that whoever was following her was likely after that information, and she couldn't let them have it. She took a deep breath, strengthened her resolve, then shoved the paper into her mouth and chomped down.

It was much harder than she'd thought it would be, chewing and breaking down and swallowing paper and ink. She had to stop herself from gagging more than once. But just in time and with tears in her eyes, she swallowed the last of it. Whoever was chasing them had entered the house, reached the door, and knew someone was inside the room. They banged on the door so loudly Maya jumped.

The pounding on the door became frequent and violent. Inari growled, ready for a fight. Although Maya shared her friend's readiness for confrontation, she didn't know how many of them there were, let alone how well she and Inari could potentially take them on. She needed to maintain the stealth advantage as much as possible before facing her attackers.

Drawing her revolver, Maya quickly pressed up against the wall next to the door. She quietly called Inari over to her. Just as the fox had made her way to her friend, the old chair gave way, and the door burst open. A young man dressed in leather entered the room. Maya wrapped her arm around the man's mouth and placed the barrel of the revolver against his back within an instant.

"Make one sound, and I won't hesitate to fire," Maya whispered.

The man, in fear for his life, did as he was told without resistance. Suddenly, a voice called out from downstairs.

"Andy, you alright up there?"

Maya guided the man inside the room as Inari quietly snarled at the voice's general direction.

"Hello, Andy," said Maya, "Now make your friend go away!"

Andy did his best to conceal his fear.

"Uh, I'm all right," he said, "Go look for her in the next house, I'll catch up when I'm done here."

"Got it!" replied the voice downstairs.

After a moment, Maya heard what sounded like another man leaving the house. Feeling assured of her situation, she forced the stranger down to his stomach.

"Inari!"

The Fox quietly sprinted towards the downed stranger and wrapped her jaws around his neck, carefully pressing her teeth against the soft flesh.

"Don't move," Maya demanded, "or she bites; hard!"

After holstering her revolver, Maya pulled out a bit of small rope from her pocket, grabbed the stranger's hands behind his back, and wrapped his wrists together. With a few feet of rope left, she connected the stranger's wrists to his ankles. Within seconds, the stranger was hogtied and immobile.

Reassured of their situation, Maya drew her revolver, placed the barrel against the strangers back, and quietly gestured her fox companion to release her grip. Inari remained close to the stranger's face, quietly growling.

"Okay, I know who you're working for, so don't play dumb with me. I just want to ask you one thing. Answer me truthfully, and maybe I'll let you live!"

The stranger had no reason to question Maya's sincerity.

"Fine, fine," replied the stranger, "what do you want to know?"

"Why is Kali following me?"

"She wants what you have. She says it has something to do with your great-aunt."

Maya had another burst of uncertain anxiety, so overwhelming that she couldn't move for a moment. *Could Kali know about the machine?* How could she? And what would she do to Maya to find it?

Whatever the course, Maya had to rethink her approach, and fast.

"All right, then. Tell me where I can find her."

23

The Meeting

Kali waited patiently for Andy and Kyle to return to camp with the captured girl. She sat on her bike, admiring the scenery of Marquam Nature Park as she waited. After a while, her thoughts began to dwell on her mother. Her most frequent memory was of her twelfth birthday. She and her friends bounced around inside a bounce-house shaped like a giant teddy bear. The backyard was covered with rainbow-colored decorations. Looking as radiant as ever, Kali's mother emerged from the house carrying the most gorgeous and delicious-looking cake she ever saw. It was one of Kali's best days from her childhood...followed by the worst.

Just before Kali lost herself entirely in the memory, she heard a strange noise coming down the path. Kali drew her knife, holding it in a combat-ready position with the blade facing downward, ready to face off against whatever might be approaching her. A moment later, much to her surprise, she saw the red fox, jumping out of the bushes, baring her teeth, and growling as she took a defensive stance.

At first, Kali was surprised; she became amused at the seemingly empty gesture from such a dumb creature. So, she changed her grip on her knife and prepared to throw it directly at Inari. When,

"I wouldn't do that!" The voice came from behind Kali. It was Maya, pointing her revolver directly at Kali's head.

"Drop the knife," she commanded.

Kali didn't like being ordered around, especially by the likes of Maya. Even so, she and her fox companion did have the upper hand, and Kali wasn't in any position to protest. So, she reluctantly dropped her knife.

Inari calmed a bit from her growling but kept her eyes on the enemy while maintaining her stance, ready to pounce if needed.

"Kick it over!" said Maya.

"You know what you're doing, kid," Kali smirked, "I'll give you that." She kicked her knife towards Maya, who carefully picked it up. "Where are my boys?"

"Don't worry, they're fine. They're just a bit tied up now. No idea when they'll be free to join us. Might be a while."

To Maya's shock, the older woman threw her head back and laughed. "Well, you're more capable than I thought!"

"Put your hands together and place them on the handlebars, now!"

Still chuckling, Kali did so.

"Inari, watch her!" This seemed to amuse the older woman even more. Maya tucked the knife into her belt and holstered the revolver. As quickly as possible, she took out a short strand of rope and tied Kali's hands to the bike's handlebars.

"I take it you don't trust me?" asked Kali.

"It's kind of hard to when your goon nearly killed my friend."

"Is that what happened? Well, I'm shocked! I never told him to hurt either of you."

"Forgive me if I find that hard to believe." Once Maya had secured Kali's hands, she backed away and took a seat at a nearby picnic area. She then took out Kali's knife and stabbed it onto the wooden table. Inari joined her once she could tell that the situation was firmly under their control.

An awkward silence fell upon the area. It felt like an eternity before it was finally broken.

"I know why you're following me," said Maya.

"Really? Because I'm not so sure myself."

"What do you know about Mae Douglass?"

"Oh, the real question, my dear, is how much do you know?"

Maya was taken aback, despite herself. "What are you talking about?"

"Honey, even the people we love the most have dark and…terrible secrets!"

She clenched her hands to keep them from shaking. "Look, lady, I'm done with puzzles right now, all right!? What are you talking about?"

Kali seemed to drift off into thought, staring into space, ignoring Maya.

"Have you ever wondered what the world was like before The Wave? What was the sudden change like for those of us who lived through it? Haven't you ever been curious about the…what did she call them…the…Days of Power?"

Maya hesitated. "Sometimes. I know the world couldn't have survived the alternative. Apparently, we were 'saved' from a terrible fate."

Suddenly, Kali bursts out into peals of laughter. Not maniacal, but genuinely amused laughter. The kind one makes when being tickled. After a moment, Kali caught her breath.

"Oh, honey, you have no idea what this is all about, do you? Your 'Auntie Dougie' didn't save lives…she destroyed them!"

Maya stared back, silently, as Kali went on.

"You weren't around when The Wave first hit the world and changed everything. Bringing us all to our knees, begging for relief. You would have been fine either way—the world you were born into was one of privilege, and a privilege that existed for generations, long before Power was vilified and made the issue. But your beloved 'auntie' didn't care about that. Neither did Clarke!"

Suddenly, Maya knew that Kali meant business. She never mentioned Dr. Clarke to Kali before, nor was there any way she could know the relevance of that name unless she was brought into the loop by Dougie. At least, that was her first thought. Kali was older than her; she had been around and would know about the world in the Days of Power. But what else could she know? More importantly, *how?*

"All right," said Maya, "let's say I believe you. What else do you know?"

A confident smile spread across Kali's face. "Take a look inside my saddlebag."

Maya stared at the saddlebag for a moment. "Inari!" She snapped her fingers, pointing at the bag, signaling the fox to give it a good sniff and search for anything dangerous. Carefully, Inari smelled the bag and everything close to it. After a moment, she seemed satisfied that there wasn't any kind of detectable threat hiding inside the bag.

"Oh, please," muttered Kali, "do I look like the booby-trap type?"

Cautiously, Maya approached the saddlebag and opened it. "What am I looking for?"

"It's wrapped in a white and blue cloth," replied Kali.

Maya searched around the inside of the saddlebag, and quickly found what she was looking for. Slowly, deliberately, she removed the bundle, and with a good deal of care, Maya unwrapped it.

It was an old journal: a faded light blue fabric cover, decorated with torn rainbow stickers and faded patches bound by a single leather cord. On the front was an elegant work of beautiful hand-stitched writing which read "Kali's Journal."

"You take that with you," said Kali, "give it a good read, then tell me I'm wrong about your precious Auntie Dougie." She sneered at the words. "I'll be here, waiting."

Maya looked at Kali. She could see the calm rage in her eyes. This was no bluff. There was something profoundly troubling inside this journal, and she wasn't sure she would like it.

Maya took the journal and went back to the picnic table. She picked up Kali's knife, walked back to her, and stabbed the blade into the ground.

"Cut yourself free if you can. I'll see you around."

With that, Maya and Inari retreated into the woods, leaving Kali alone to retrieve her knife however she could.

"Smart kid," Kali proclaimed to herself as she quickly removed the handlebars from the bike with a few simple twists, before retrieving her knife to cut the ropes.

24

Kali's Journal

Maya and Inari returned to the abandoned general store where they camped out on their first night inside the city. Much to her relief, The Beast was still in its hiding place, untouched. After making their way inside, Maya poured a bowl of water for Inari and opened a can of food for her.

As Maya munched on some trail mix for herself, she examined the old journal. She wasn't sure what she would find written inside, but she had a feeling that whatever it was, it couldn't be good.

Maya took a deep breath and opened the book to where it was marked with the small fabric ribbon.

May 14, 2037 – 5:04 PM

I had my 12th birthday today. It was lots of fun. Mom set

up one of those bouncy houses for all of us. My favorite present was the wood-burning kit Grandpa gave me. He promised he would show me how to use it and make some beautiful designs on my desk. He also gave me an old watch he once got as a graduation gift. It tells the time and date without batteries. I must remember to wind it. I can't wait for him to come back and visit again.

May 15, 2037 - 7:23 PM

The power went out all around the house today. It looks like the whole town has a blackout. I wasn't scared, neither was mom. We set up candles and had dinner. Mom used a lighter to turn the stove on and made me ham and eggs for dinner tonight. I liked that. I asked her if she knew when the lights might come back on, but she didn't know. Dad was busy trying to fix the problem. I hope the lights come back on soon.

May 18, 2037 - 8:42 PM

It's been three days since we lost the power. Mom is starting to get worried. She and Dad were fighting today. Grandpa was supposed to come and visit today, but he didn't show up yet. I hope he's okay. I'm starting to get a little scared.

May 23, 2037 – 4:39 PM

Some people tried to break into our house today. They wanted to steal our food. We don't have a lot right now. They forced their way inside. Dad tried to fight them but he got hurt. Mom says it's getting too dangerous to stay here, and we may have to leave. I don't know where we will go. I hope we go to Grandpa's.

May 24, 2037 – 10:12 AM

Dad is dead. Mom says he tried hard to stay. He said he loved Mom and me very much. Why is all of this happening?

May 25, 2037 - 6:12 PM

Mom and I picked up a few things, and we walked out of the house. She had to fight off some strangers as we walked. We hiked most of the day and camped outside. Mom told me that we were going to Grandpa's place. She says it will be safe there.

"Oh, Kali," said Maya to herself.

May 28, 2037 – 2:27 PM

Mom and I are at Grandpa's house, but he isn't here. We searched all over, but all we found was a note from Grandpa's best friend, Mae Dougie.

A sudden chill ran down Maya's spine.

As she continued to read the journal, she gained a greater understanding of Kali's position. The journal described how Dougie instructed Kali and her mother to go to her brother's farm in Shasta. They were on their way and stopped by the area that would eventually become The Trade Post. Before it became the bustling town it was today, it was a tiny open village populated mainly by former city folk—people who had not yet adjusted to the sudden new way of life.

Kali's mother would participate in forming their town, using the nearby water as trade. She would rebuild a small city for those who needed that sort of environment to survive. A life on Dougie's farm would have to wait.

Eventually, Kali and her mother became too entrenched in the creation and maintenance of their little city; they never made it to Dougie's. It wasn't until years later that Dougie stumbled upon The Trade Post on her earlier journeys to maintain the machine. That night, as they were treating Dougie to dinner, Kali's mother asked her to go to her room while she and Dougie discussed some "important business." Kali did as she was asked and left the table, but never made it to her room.

Instead, Kali ran around the corner and hid there so she could listen in on their conversation out of wild curiosity. That very night, Kali learned of her grandfather's actions and how the world went dark. How the man she'd loved, who had given her his precious watch, had turned off the lights and then murdered himself, alone in a cold laboratory next to the tangle of metal that was his greatest achievement and the world's most insidious weapon. At that moment, she began to despise her grandfather, despite how much she loved him before. She blamed him for the death of her father, and the whole world being turned upside-down, and the constant fear of other people.

And no real future to call her own. Maya felt this, too, most keenly.

Maya was stunned by everything in this little blue journal. She suddenly had a much more profound understanding of what Kali wanted: she wanted to take control of the machine!

25

The Question

After reading through the rest of Kali's journal, Maya understood Kali better than she ever thought. Learning of her hardships during the early days of The Wave, discovering the terrible things she had had to face, including her father's death, made Maya think twice about her stance on the state of the world as she knew it. Maya was born into this world with no knowledge of the Days of Power, outside of stories and shared memories. Her heart was heavy, and she thought, yet again, *why send me? Why, Dougie? Why did you do this? Why?*

She just sat there, paralyzed, journal in her hands, dumbfounded and exhausted. She realized that the choice was now before her: she could complete her great aunt's original mission or take a chance with Kali, returning the world to the Days of Power.

On the one hand, the world seemed to function well the way it was now. According to Dougie, their actions had saved humanity from a terrible disaster. And people seemed to adapt well enough…at least the people Maya knew. But then, Maya realized, she only knew the people in her home village. They'd all come from nearby towns where they had homes, and clothes, and plenty of food and resources…for them, turning off the power was a hardship but not a death sentence. *But what about the others,* she thought. *Not everyone has what we have. They died because of The Wave, and they weren't a threat to anyone.* Dougie and Clarke's "new world" came at the price of denying a whole generation the freedom to choose their destiny. They were forced out of their world and deprived of a voice. Instead, the future was handed to them whether they wanted it or not. And so many innocent people were left to die, without consideration or care. Because someone had decided to play God.

Maya paced the room, collecting her thoughts, scanning through Kali's journal when a faint voice suddenly stopped her.

"Overwhelming, isn't it?"

With a flash, Maya turned and faced the intruder, drawing her revolver. Kali stood near the doorway, with her arms crossed against her chest.

"How did you…,"

"I've got more tricks up my sleeve than you know, little girl."

An uncomfortable pause filled the room.

"In case you're wondering," said Kali, "I'm here alone. I promise."

"Why should I believe you? You've been lying to me from the start!"

Kali bristled at this. "I never lied to you, little girl. I merely didn't share everything. I was up front with my knowledge of your great aunt, wasn't I?"

Maya glared, but did not reply.

"Look, would you please put down the gun? It's hard to have a conversation like this."

Maya thought about it for a moment before gently placing the revolver on the ground, as a gesture of good faith.

"Inari, if she moves, you know what to do."

Inari settled into a ready-to-pounce position.

"I must say," said Kali, "that guard fox of yours is something else."

Maya kept her eyes on Kali.

"Okay," said Maya, "here's how this is going to go down. I'll ask you one question. If I like your answer, I will take you to The Machine, and we can move on from there together. If I don't like your answer, then I will make sure that you never find it. Are we clear?"

"So diplomatic," said Kali, dryly. "I love it."

"Are we clear?" repeated Maya.

"Yes," replied Kali. "Crystal."

Maya took a deep breath before she presented her question. "What do you want with The Machine?"

An uncomfortable silence filled the room. Kali just stood there: staring, incredulous, motionless. "You know what I want."

Suddenly, Inari sensed something dangerous just behind them, and she barked in that direction. Maya turned to look, and lost focus.

"Damn it!" cried Kali as she reached for her six-shooter. Upon hearing Kali's frustrated cry, Maya turned back to see Kali drawing her weapon. Kali may have been quick, but Maya was quicker. She shot her hidden blade towards Kali with a quick flick of the wrist, striking her right in the forearm and forcing her to drop her gun to the ground.

"Come on!" cried Maya, as she and Inari ran down the hallway and towards the back exit of the building. They were in such a hurry to get out of there that Maya realized all too late she had forgotten the revolver, still lying on the ground.

As Kali fell to her knees in pain from the short blade in her arm, her men bolted through the windows, ready to grab Maya, surprised to find she wasn't in position. One of them noticed Kali on the ground and ran over to her.

"You all right, boss?"

"I'll be fine," she said through her teeth, "get after them! Bring the girl alive."

He pointed at his companion.

"You go! I'll take care of Kali!"

The other acknowledged, and ran in the direction of the girl and the fox.

26

The Flames Grew Higher

They ran through the abandoned city in the dead of night. Maya could barely make out her own hands before her, let alone determine which direction she was going. She tried her best to follow where she thought she could hear Inari running, but kept tripping and stumbling over unseen obstacles.

Finally, Inari ran back to her friend, stood directly in front of her, then quickly turned around with her tail sticking straight up into the air. Inari remained in that position, waiting for something, though Maya could not quite understand what she was doing at first—not helped by the sounds of Kali's henchman hot on their trail.

Maya remembered suddenly that foxes have incredible night vision. Was Inari signaling to Maya that she could guide her through the darkness? Carefully, and with a bit of hesitation, Maya took hold of Inari's tail. Almost immediately, Inari bolted from their spot, guiding Maya through the night. It was the strangest thing Maya had ever experienced…and the most exciting.

As the two of them made their way through the city, the fox scanned the area for an excellent place to hide, with Maya holding her tail. After a moment, she found the perfect spot: near the old city road were many overgrown bushes, with spaces just big enough for them to enter and hide. Inari guided Maya through the twigs and leaves until they found themselves in a small clearing within the bushes, just big enough for the two of them.

Maya kneeled before her friend and held onto her for dear life. "Thank you," she whispered. "How are you so clever?" A moment later, she noticed a small burst of flame emanating from the direction they came. It was their pursuer, lighting a torch. It didn't cast much light, but it was still big enough to be noticed through the bushes. Maya and Inari remained as still and quiet as possible, hoping that this goon would pass them by without noticing their position.

"Come on out, little girl!" he called. "You can't hide forever!"

Maya could see how far away the flame was. It was at least a hundred yards away from their position in the bushes. She thought as quickly as she could.

"Okay, wait here," said Maya to her friend. "I'll be back, I promise."

Inari did as she was told, while Maya snuck out of the bushes.

She carefully felt her way around the area, keeping her eyes on the incoming flame. She stayed low and behind cover when she could find it. She stalked the torch, and observed its pattern like she was hunting.

The man, meanwhile, searched high and low for them. He held his torch as far out as he could reach, his knife in his other hand, ready for an attack.

The area was so dark that he didn't notice Maya hiding behind a large pole as he walked. The moment he passed, she moved in and grabbed him from behind, forcing him to drop the torch on the ground, setting a nearby bush ablaze.

The goon quickly turned around, freeing himself from Maya's grip as he tried to swing at her with his knife. She moved away like a flash, dodging the swing. She drew her own knife. The two of them stood before each other, waiting to make the first move.

"We don't have to do this," said Maya, quietly.

"No," he spat back, "but you're making me angry, and I don't care what the boss says anymore!"

Suddenly, he swung hard at Maya, only for her to dodge yet again. Occasionally their blades would clash and strike sparks in the night. As the nearby flames grew higher, so did the intensity of their fight. Soon the fire grew taller and taller until it could be seen from at least a mile away.

The goon was somewhat formidable at knife fighting. Maya spent most of the fight trying to tire him out, doing her best to avoid taking him down. To her dismay, he didn't share that mentality—he was out to kill, his orders to take her alive be damned.

After several swipes and dodges, Maya decided it was finally time to end this. She waited for the opportune moment. Just as the goon was about to move in and strike at Maya's chest, she rolled along his arm and stabbed her blade right into the back of his neck, killing him in a matter of seconds.

"I'm sorry," said Maya, as the man fell to the ground, dead.

As the flames continued to grow, Inari burst out of the bushes and ran towards Maya, who was rather worse for wear and more than a little bloodied. She fell to her knees and held onto her friend tightly.

"It's all right, girl," said Maya. "Come on, we have to get out of here."

And with that, the two of them escaped into the night once again.

27

The Next Step

Kali rested on the ground while Andy, her last man alive, tended to her wound. The thin blade had made its way clean through her forearm, its ends sticking out on either side. By sheer luck, it missed any critical arteries.

"I have to take it out," said Andy.

Kali reached into her pocket with her other arm and pulled out a bandana. She bunched it up into a ball and stuffed it in her mouth before signaling that she was ready. With due care, Andy took a firm grip on the flat end of the blade.

"I'll count to three," he said.

Kali nodded.

"One—"

Suddenly, Andy yanked the blade right out of Kali's forearm, causing her to scream in pain through the cloth stuffed inside her mouth. As Kali continued to make muffled grunts and screams, Andy cleaned the wound and wrapped it up in a bandage. Once Kali had calmed down, she ripped the cloth out of her jaws.

"God damn it!" she proclaimed.

"I'm sorry," Andy said lamely. "I knew it was going to hurt." After ensuring his boss was all right, he looked towards the route their prey had taken, along with his cohort. "You want me to see if he's found her yet?"

"No," replied Kali, "we go together."

"Are you sure you can move?"

"It's an arm, not a leg!"

The two of them tried to follow Maya's trail, using their torch for light. Within minutes, Kali saw the burning brush in the distance. As they approached the pile of scorched leaves and twigs, they found their companion, lying dead on the ground.

"Kyle!" called the last man, as he rushed over.

"Andy," said Kali, exhausted, "don't bother. He's dead."

Andy's agitation quickly turned to rage. "That little bitch!" he cried. "Why the hell would she kill him? He was going to take her alive! She didn't try to kill us before!"

Kali rolled her eyes. "We did ambush her," she said. "She tried to test me. Trying to see if I was 'worthy' of her little secret."

"What did she say?"

"She asked me what I wanted with The Machine. The two of you burst onto the scene before I could answer."

"Were you even going to give her an answer?"

"Not one she would have wanted to hear."

She turned away from him as she processed a thought.

"She won't trust me with another chance now. She'll sooner take us down than share what she knows."

"So?" said Andy. "What do we do now?"

Kali thought quickly.

"Do you remember exactly where you were when you last encountered her?" asked Kali.

"Yeah."

"Well, something tells me we'll find her there again. Let's get moving!"

With that, the two of them made their way back to where Andy had first encountered Maya and her fox friend. As they approached the street where they first saw Maya scaling the uphill road, Kali had a moment of realization.

"Of course," she said to herself.

"What is it?" asked Andy.

"This is where it all began for me. My grandfather's house is just up this hill. I haven't been back here in ages."

Andy looked confused, wondering what any of this had to do with their mission.

"Forgive me, boss, but why is that important right now?" asked Andy.

"Oh, trust me, it's imperative," replied Kali. "It's so important that I need to make sure it remains so."

Andy became a bit uneven, suddenly nervous. "All right…how?"

"By ensuring that fewer people know about the significance of this place."

"Fewer?"

Kali drew her old six-shooter with her uninjured arm, shooting Andy as he stood befuddled. "Sorry, darling. You've been a tremendous help." And with that, there was only Kali and her determination.

"All right, little girl," said Kali to herself, "it's just you and me now."

28

Lead The Way

The gunshot echoed around Maya and Inari as they both looked up, searching for the source. Maya knew that it was a gunshot and figured it was most likely from Kali's six-shooter, but had no way of being sure. More importantly, it was far away from their current position, so she wasn't overly concerned about it. Not yet, anyway.

They made their way further into the city and found a new place to hide and make camp for the night. After tending to her minor wounds, she and Inari had a little supper and tucked themselves in for the night. Occasionally, during her fitful and anxious sleep, Maya would briefly wake and, for just a few seconds before dozing off again, see the fox standing guard over her as she slept. She wondered if Inari slept at all. If she did, it must have been whenever Maya wasn't looking.

The next morning, Maya was determined to finally complete her mission. Even with Kali out there, she knew that it needed to be done. She needed to see this incredible machine for herself. She just had to make her way to it as carefully as possible, and not run into her pursuers again.

Maya decided to first head back to their original hiding place to retrieve the revolver. Although it was a risk, she felt it was a necessary one. If she was going to face-off against Kali again, she wanted to be prepared.

The two of them carefully snuck back to the old store, winding and weaving in all different directions to avoid easy detection. After a while, they reached their old hiding place. Maya peeked through a window and searched for signs of Kali or her other goon. None could be detected.

Cautiously, Maya made her way inside with Inari right behind her. She gauged the fox's behavior at their surroundings and was relieved to see that Inari didn't sense any immediate threats. As Maya searched the area, she was relieved to find The Beast exactly where she had left it the night before; still intact with no parts or items missing.

Also, much to her relief, the revolver was still resting on the ground, right where she left it. She opened the cylinder, loaded a few fresh bullets, and holstered it. Now she was ready to complete her mission.

Hastily and with no small amount of care, they headed back toward their intended destination. Maya surveyed the area to determine a less direct approach that would make it easier to sneak past anyone who might be on the lookout for them. After an hour or two of hiking, climbing, and zigzagging all over the area, they finally reached the strange clay-looking house. Bright orange with oddly shaped windows, just like she remembered from the drawing before she'd destroyed it.

After a quick sweep of the area and consulting Inari's instincts, they both felt assured of their situation and made their way inside. Far enough away, unseen and unnoticed by Inari, Kali watched silently as they entered the house.

Time had not been kind to the place; years' worth of neglect showed on all the dusty surfaces. Broken windows lined with washed-out paint along the edges, likely from years of rainfall making its way inside. Signs of squatters and campers using the space from time to time. Empty food containers and makeshift beds out of every piece of furniture around the place, not to mention the uncomfortable signs of past violence—Maya saw bloodstains on one wall.

"Okay," she whispered, "where is that thing?" She searched through her memory and recalled Dougie's drawing and scanned the area. She made her way to the kitchen and carefully glided her hands along the walls, searching for the hidden button. Inari stood by and watched in befuddlement. "I know," Maya commented, "this looks silly, doesn't it?"

The fox tilted her head as if in response.

After several minutes of sliding her hands on the walls, she felt something unusual. Her fingers pressed a hard metallic shape, and she was greeted by the sudden sound of gears turning from across the room. Inari jumped at the sound and bolted towards Maya, ready to defend her friend from whatever danger might emerge. Much to their mutual relief and amazement, the noise turned out to be an elaborate clockwork mechanism, opening a secret passageway hidden behind a tall metallic box in the kitchen. *Refrigerator*, Maya recalled, the device was referred to as a refrigerator back in the Days of Power.

Maya carefully approached the dark passageway. She could see stairs, and she knew they had to go down them. Inari whimpered at the sight, not liking the idea at all.

"It's all right, girl," said Maya trying to comfort her friend. "Don't worry. I've got your back, and you've got mine. We'll be okay."

And with that, the two of them made their way down the dark and ominous passageway, with Kali, unbeknownst to them, not far behind.

29

Confrontation

They carefully descended the stairs, their eyes slowly adjusting to the dark. Much to their relief, the descent was not all that deep, maybc fifteen feet. Once they reached the bottom, they found another short hallway leading to what appeared to be a light source. But…it wasn't daylight or candlelight. This was something *different*, something she had never seen before. It was a strange white light that seemed to illuminate the entire room down the hallway. And there was a frightful hum emanating from the room.

Maya looked at Inari, who appeared concerned but not afraid to venture down the dark hallway with her friend.

"This is it," she said, "it's now or never!"

They moved closer to the bright room, and the hum grew louder. Maya could feel the pulses resonate in her chest. Inari kept her eyes moving, making sure to be fully prepared to tackle anything they might encounter. After what felt like a stroll through molasses, Maya and Inari reached the bright room.

And there it was.

In the center of the room, glowing like a white-hot star, was The Machine. It was more ominous and fascinating than Maya could have imagined. For a moment, Maya was amazed at the sight of this giant of technology. This very thing had made the world as Maya understood it.

Is that really what Power looks like? she asked herself.

As Maya gazed upon the glowing wonder, something caught Inari's eye, and she ran over to investigate. Maya was so engrossed at the unusual light from the machine that she didn't notice the fox had run off. It wasn't until she barked loudly that the girl finally snapped out of her trance and rushed over to see what the fuss was all about. Inari stood beside a small desk and chair covered with dust and what looked like old bloodstains. The desk had a square-shaped glass that looked directly at whoever was sitting in the chair. In front of the glass was a row of buttons with letters and numbers. It reminded Maya of Dougie's typewriter, but nothing happened when she hit some of the buttons. She wondered where the hammers and paper were.

Inari nuzzled up against one of the desk's drawers, trying to open it, prompting Maya to do so herself. Inside was a new manila envelope, with her name written on the front, in Dougie's handwriting. Carefully, she took the envelope from the drawer, opened it, and removed the contents. Inside was another, and likely the last, typewritten letter from Dougie. It read:

My dear Maya,

By now you will have reached your ultimate destination, and come face to face with The Machine. This is the life's work of my dear friend, Dr. Clarke. He gave his life for humanity.

Now, it is at this junction that I must apologize. For you see, I have not been entirely honest with you. No maintenance is required for the machine. Dr. Clarke's design ensures its infinite longevity. Though it is not indestructible, it is capable of prolonged self-maintenance.

Please do not despair, for I was still truthful about something far more important. When I told you that your generation needed to decide for itself what future they will build, I meant that exactly.

This is the true task I have given you.

With this final letter, I have enclosed the key you will need to decode my instructions for accessing the machine. Once you have completed the required sequence, you will have complete control and, if you so choose, you may reverse the effects of The Wave.

The choice is yours, my dear. You have seen the world as it has become on your travels. You alone have the wisdom and the knowledge to decide where humanity will go from here. I have faith in your courage, wisdom, and ability.

Whatever you choose, know that I have always loved you like a daughter, and wherever I may be at this moment, I will be forever proud of you.

The time has come, my dear. Make the choice.

Love,
Dougie

"I knew it," she said to herself.

Suddenly, the familiar clicking sound of a gun's hammer pulling back echoed throughout the room.

Maya ducked behind cover, a mere fraction of a second before a shot was fired in their direction.

"You knew, and still you came," Kali said acidly. "You came for the same reason she and the good doctor did all this in the first place. Glory. Entitlement. Ownership. It wasn't the electrical Power they wanted to control. It was power over humankind. It drove them mad, and it murdered my grandfather."

As she spoke, Maya held Inari close as she struggled to run out and attack. "Easy, girl," she whispered. After a moment, the fox calmed down and remained at her friend's side. Maya drew her revolver, checked to ensure it was loaded, then held it in a ready position.

"I think you should stay right where you are," said Maya, "I've got a gun also."

Maya reached her arm over the cover and blindly aimed where Kali was likely standing, firing a warning shot. Kali, completely surprised, jumped and fell to the ground for cover.

"Okay," she said, "I think we understand each other."

An awkward moment of silence permeated throughout the room until Maya finally broke it.

"If you're looking for how to operate the machine, I have the only written instructions with me for how to do it. There is no other way of controlling this thing."

"What makes you think I want to control it?"

"Because I've read your journal, Kali. I know all about you. Your parents, the things you've had to endure, and who you blame for it!"

Kali fired her six-shooter in Maya's direction. Maya fired back.

Suddenly, as the bullets flew overhead, Inari broke away from Maya, quietly making her way towards Kali for a sneak attack.

Maya tried to call her back silently, but it was too late.

"You can't hide there forever, little girl," said Kali.

"Who says I'm hiding," replied Maya, "and stop calling me 'little girl!'"

Like a flash of red lightning, Inari pounced, clamping her jaws onto Kali's arm with the gun. Maya frantically jumped out and bolted towards her enemy. Kali struggled against the fox's sharp grasp. Within an instant, Maya took her free hand and jammed her fingers into a few spots on the woman's back. Kali fell forward, completely immobile.

"Pressure Points," exclaimed Maya!

Kali struggled and squirmed.

Inari kept her eyes on the enemy, ready to attack at a moment's notice. Maya picked up the six-shooter. She carefully picked Kali up and leaned her back against the desk. Once Kali was in a seated position, Maya sat down on the floor right across from her.

"You never answered my question," she said.

Kali was utterly dumbfounded.

"Like it or not," Maya continued, "we are both part of this dilemma—"

"There is no dilemma," exclaimed Kali, "there never was! There is only what my grandfather did to us because of his stupid and misguided sense of self-righteousness! What, you think he saved lives with that thing over there? No! He destroyed them! He broke the world!!! How could you even begin to understand? You weren't here when it all started. You weren't here when everyone lost their minds! When we had to fight, just to see the next day! My grandfather was wrong! He didn't fix anything!"

Silence.

"No, he didn't," replied Maya simply. "You're right. I could never know what you went through, and I'm sorry…for everything."

Maya's feelings started to overwhelm her as tears ran down her face.

"You know why I decided to take this journey?" asked Maya.

"To stop me," replied Kali.

"No. I can't."

A confused look rolled across Kali's face.

"What are you saying?"

Maya gazed at the Machine across the room as it hummed.

"What Dr. Clarke did is unforgivable! No matter how noble his intentions were, no matter how much of a bleaker future he saved us from, no one should ever believe that he had the right to balance or justify any loss of life like he did."

Maya stopped to catch her breath.

"I think," she continued, "deep down, Dougie knew that."

Maya turned her attention to Kali.

"I think, through all of the lies and philosophizing, she's been trying to…to make amends for his actions. But I may never forgive Dr. Clarke. I know you never will, and I understand."

Maya now had Kali's full attention.

"Before I left home," Maya continued, "Dougie told me that I had to make the choice for my generation, to keep the power off or bring it back. But I can't do that. Not by myself."

Kali was dumbfounded.

"What do you mean?"

Maya turned to look at her friend. Inari stared back with a glance that felt…reassuring.

"This is no longer my choice to make," said Maya as she turned to look Kali right in the eye, "…it's yours."

Kali was taken aback as if struck by lightning.

"I may not like how my world came to be," Maya continued, "but it's still mine. And for better or worse, I have happiness here. I am fortunate enough to live in a world that I can share with the people I love. But, this isn't your world. No, your world was taken from you. And I may never be able to make that right."

Gently, like drops of early rain, tears fell from Kali's eyes.

"Even so," Maya continued, "that doesn't mean I shouldn't try."

Maya stood up, approached Kali, withdrew her six-shooter, and placed it inside Kali's hand. Ever so gently, she tapped a few areas on Kali's body with her fingers. When she was done, she turned her attention over to Inari.

"Listen, girl. I want you to go upstairs. No matter what you hear, don't come back down. You stay up there until one or both of us comes back up. You understand?"

The fox whined unease at this order.

"Hey, don't worry, it'll be all right. I promise."

Maya embraced her friend with all the love she could muster. Kali watched in amazement.

"I love you so much. Thank you…for everything. Now, please…go."

Slowly, sadly, Inari did as she was told, and shuffled her way back down the dark hallway towards the stairs.

Maya returned to her seated position across from Kali.

"In a few minutes," she said, "you will start to regain feeling in your body. When you do, you will have a choice: you can either complete your mission by taking control of the machine and restoring power to the world, while you take your revenge on me, and only me, or you and I can work together, and find a better solution."

Kali felt overwhelmed, as if she were suddenly covered by a warm blanket on a cold winter night.

"Why," she replied. "Why don't you just kill me?"

"Because that's what the old world would want. No one trusting anyone, everyone just arguing and fighting over petty differences. Blaming each other for our problems instead of blaming those who are truly at fault. If we're going to be the voice of humanity, and right now we kind of are, then we need to do better. I need to do better! All I'm asking for is a chance to…to earn your trust, and make things right, however I can. Maybe you don't believe me, maybe you're not sure, but you won't know, unless you try."

The two women faced off each other, tears and uncertainty filling their eyes.

"I may have made a promise," Maya continued, "but the only thing worse than breaking a promise, is keeping one you probably shouldn't have made."

Kali began to feel her fingers again. As she regained feeling in her hand, she gripped the handle of her six-shooter tightly. Maya remained in her seated position, motionless and unflinching. The hum of the machine seemed to grow and overtake the room.

As Kali regained more feeling in her arm, she lifted her thumb, and pulled back the hammer.

30

There and Back Again

It was a calm day at Douglass Ranch, with people working, playing, and preparing for the upcoming summer. Dougie was in the middle of another Story-time session with the children, including Maya's little brother, Charlie. Today's story was one of Dougie's favorites: *The Hobbit* by J.R.R. Tolkien, also one of Charlie's favorites. The children listened with wonder as Dougie read:

"'You are a wonderful person, Mr. Baggins, and I am very fond of you, but you are only quite a little fellow in a wide world after all!' 'Thank goodness!' said Bilbo laughing'"

Dougie opted to skip the very last sentence.

"The end," she said.

The children erupted with joy and gratitude for another special story-time with the old woman. Charlie was especially fond of this time with her.

"All right now, children, it's time for chores."

There was a collective sigh across the room.

"Come now, none of that, let's get going. It'll be just as fun, I promise."

The children reluctantly got up from their seated positions and headed out the door to go about their various assigned tasks—all except for Charlie, who stayed behind.

"Auntie Dougie," he said, "do you think Maya is coming home today?"

Dougie placed her hand on Charlie's shoulder. "Oh, my dear little one, I wish I could tell you, but I…"

Suddenly, Dougie was distracted by something. She turned her attention towards the window. Charlie looked up at Dougie, somewhat confused.

"What is it?" asked Charlie.

"Listen," replied Dougie, "can you hear that?"

Charlie concentrated his hearing. After a moment, he thought he could hear something strange. Something that sounded mechanical and moving fast towards their village.

"Is that…," said Charlie.

Dougie looked at Charlie with a hopeful smile as if to say, *I think so!* With a shot of excitement, little Charlie ran out the door and towards the approximate location of the noise. Dougie followed as close behind as she could, despite the hindrance of her cane.

Charlie was out of the house and at the village's gate next to the old road within seconds. Joseph, while hammering a piece of orange-hot metal, noticed Charlie by the gate with Dougie seemingly in pursuit. Out of curiosity and concern, Joseph placed the hot metal piece in water and sprinted towards Dougie to find out what was happening.

"What's going on, Dougie?" asked Joseph.

"I don't know yet," replied Dougie.

Joseph heard the noise as well. He ran over to Charlie to see what he saw and make sure he'd be safe from whatever was coming. The two of them stared down the road as the noise grew louder and closer. Emerging just over the horizon, they saw her.

It was Maya! She and Inari had made it home on The Beast.

"Maya!" shouted Charlie as he ran towards her.

Maya stopped her ride, hopped off, and ran straight towards her little brother. Inari jumped out of the passenger seat and followed her friend. Seconds later, Maya scooped up her little brother and held him tighter and with more love than ever before.

"Charlie!" she said with tears of joy in her eyes, "Oh, I missed you so much!"

Maya fell to her knees with Charlie wrapped up tightly in her arms. She smothered him with kisses and kept parting his hair to see his face.

"You're back!" proclaimed Charlie.

"I told you, I would always come back," replied Maya.

Suddenly, a gentle bark emanated from behind. Maya turned around and saw Inari sitting patiently close by as if waiting to meet her little brother. Charlie was a bit nervous at first, having never seen a fox this close before.

"It's all right," said Maya.

She placed him down on the ground and stepped back a bit.

"Charlie, say hello to my friend, Inari. She took care of me out there."

Charlie hesitated for a moment. Inari worked her magic and waved her paw towards him as she lowered her head. Cautiously, Charlie approached Inari with his hand extended, palm up. Once he was close enough, Inari took a few sniffs, then licked his hand as her tail wagged in excitement. Feeling more assured of her gentle nature, Charlie patted Inari on the head, prompting Inari to step forward and lick his face. Charlie burst out in joyful laughter as he continued to pet his new friend.

"Nice to see you weren't alone," said Joseph as he approached.

Maya looked at Joseph deep in the eyes before embracing him with incredible gratitude.

"Thank you for looking after him," said Maya.

"Come on," said Joseph, "Dougie is eager to see you."

As they made their way to the village entrance, Maya could see her great-aunt waiting patiently by the gate. Suddenly, the village's dogs caught wind of Maya's scent and raced out the gate to greet her. They hesitated when they saw Inari by her side, but after a few exchanges of howls and barks and sniffs, they seemed to accept Maya's new companion as one of their own.

Maya walked up to Dougie, uncertain of what to do.

"My dear," said Dougie, "I…"

Before she could phrase her sentence, Maya instantly wrapped her arms around her great-aunt, without saying a word.

As quickly as the embrace began, Maya released her grip and walked directly inside the house.

Dougie stood by and wondered.

31

Bittersweet

That night, after the whole village exhausted themselves celebrating Maya's return, a deep quiet fell upon the air unlike any other before. As Maya checked around the house for the night, she peeked through her little brother's bedroom door to check on him. He was fast asleep, with Inari curled up into a ball at the foot of his bed. Maya admired the beautiful sight before her, comforted that she was home again with her loved ones. Carefully, she closed the door, leaving it slightly cracked.

Maya stepped into the kitchen and sat down at the table, alone with her thoughts. A moment later, Dougie entered the kitchen.

"Oh, hello my dear," she said.

Maya didn't answer.

"Listen, I know that…"

"Please," Maya interrupted, "stop talking."

Dougie stood in place, almost petrified of what might follow.

"Sit down."

Carefully, Dougie sat across from Maya, her hands trembling.

"Do you remember," said Maya, "what you told me the day I left?"

Dougie seemed a bit dumbfounded.

"Of course," she replied, "you had to make the choice for yourself."

"That's not what I'm talking about."

Silence.

"When I left," Maya continued, "I thought it was to undo what you and Dr. Clarke did together. I believed you were as directly responsible as he was. Then, I remembered something else. You said,

'When *Dr. Clarke* made his choice' and not 'when *we* made the choice.' At first, I thought you were trying to distance yourself from your actions. But then, I started thinking about everything else a bit differently."

Dougie knew exactly where this was going, and she wasn't comfortable about it.

"So please," continued Maya, "tell me the truth. What really happened that day?"

There was no avoiding this discussion now. Despite her reservations, Dougie took a deep breath, and told her story to her great-niece.

First, she discussed how she came to work with and eventually admire Dr. Clarke as a fellow scientist. Her passion for unraveling the human condition, combined with his desire for massive global impact, made them the perfect storm of possibilities. Her expertise in chaos theory provided significant data pertaining to The Machine, and its impact on the world. Dr. Clarke believed she was the right person to answer his many inquiries.

Even so, Dougie didn't believe that Dr. Clarke would ever really use it. She believed the whole thing was nothing more than a mere thought experiment given physical form.

She told Maya about the day of The Wave. How she tried to stop Dr. Clarke from doing what he did, how she felt betrayed by someone she loved and admired for so long. She has carried that anger with her ever since.

"You loved him?" asked Maya.

Dougie shook her head.

"Not like that," she replied. "He was like a father to me. He believed in me when no one else would. He gave me the chance to become a part of something greater than myself. To have an impact on the world. I just never wanted it to be…this."

Maya's mind was racing with a million thoughts and questions, struggling to find the right words.

"Why didn't you just take control of The Machine and undo the damage yourself?" asked Maya. "You knew how."

"You're right, I did know how, and I tried…once before."

Instantly, Maya wanted to chew out her great-aunt. She could have reversed The Wave herself, and yet she sent her great-niece on a seemingly wild goose chase? She was ready to read Dougie the riot act. But, before any words could escape her, she pulled herself back, realizing there must be more to that statement than its face value.

Despite her feelings, Maya continued to listen.

Dougie continued to relay her story. Telling Maya about traveling from the lab to her brother's ranch in Shasta — *Douglass Ranch* — how she felt the need to get as far away from there as possible. She spent her life establishing the village with her family, helping people grow and find a new life for themselves in the aftermath of the great change. Trying to make amends for her mentors' drastic actions the best she could.

After some time, she decided to venture back to the secret lab, and at least try to make things right by reversing the effects of The Wave.

When Dougie arrived, she knew the door was locked. she contemplated ways of breaking in. But, for some incomprehensible reason, Dougie was inspired to simply try the combination last used. Naturally, she assumed Dr. Clarke had changed it, wanting to prevent her from ever entering that place again, and reversing his choice. But, as Dougie turned that dial, using the exact combination she recalled, much to her surprise, the door swung open.

"I still remember the smell," said Dougie. "It was like a fish market."

Having gained access to the lab, and upon discovering Dr. Clarke's remains, she took his body outside and cremated it. She returned to the lab, fully prepared to access The Machine, and reverse the effects of The Wave. Then, she was struck with an epiphany.

Why didn't Dr. Clarke change the combination, she thought to herself. *Unless…*

"He wanted me to return."

An uncertain silence fell upon the room.

"Dr. Clarke and I both knew," Dougie continued, "that nothing could ever justify using The Machine. No matter how bleak everything became, we could not, in good conscience, force the world to change like The Wave did. I like to think…even after pushing that button…he still knew that. He had accepted the consequences of his actions, and wanted me to decide where humanity goes from here."

"So, why didn't you?" asked Maya.

"Because, as I said before, it was no longer my choice to make. It needed to be yours."

Dougie could no longer hold back the tears forcing their way down her face.

"I will never forgive Dr. Clarke for his selfishness," Dougie continued, "but…it gave me a better future. It gave me you, light of my life."

Maya stared at her great-aunt, not reacting to the tears in her own eyes.

"If I had made the choice for you," Dougie continued, "I might have become the monster Dr. Clarke was fighting…and became. You are the future, my dear. I couldn't take that away from you."

As Maya looked at her great-aunt, she felt an overwhelming sense of empathy she had never expected. Without even thinking about it, she stood up, approached Dougie, and embraced her tightly. Dougie held onto Maya for dear life.

"You're not a monster," said Maya softly, "you never were."

Dougie cried silently into Maya's chest.

"You sent me away with an old saying," continued Maya, "now, I have one for you. 'Accept the things to which fate binds you, and love the people with whom fate brings you together, but do so with all your heart.'"

Dougie looked up at Maya with a smile, eyes red from the tears.

"Marcus Aurelius," she said.

"That," said Maya, "is your legacy, and yours alone."

Slowly, gracefully, the two women smiled at each other, with more love in their hearts than ever before. As they held each other, basking in their warmth, Inari looked on from behind the cracked bedroom door. She seemed to admire the view before her, as she felt her best friend's profound sense of peace. In that moment, she saw Maya's light shine like the warm morning sun.

Epilogue

The Visitor

It had been three months since Maya's triumphant return. In that time, Inari became fast friends with the whole village, especially with the children. She loved to play with them every chance she got, especially Charlie.

Maya would occasionally tell stories of her travels at special events in the village, with a few creative embellishments and omissions, of course. She never told Dougie about her encounter with Kali. Maybe she would when the time was right. At least, that's what Maya felt was best.

A delightful surprise came in the form of an unexpected visit from Michael and Izzy. Dougie was grateful to see her friend, and Inari was ecstatic to play with little Izzy once again, a joy that few others could match.

Dougie retired from her position as village leader allowing Maya to take her place. Maya proved herself to be just as good a resource to the village as Dougie before her. All seemed well in her little corner of the world.

One day, at around 2:00 in the afternoon, it happened. As Maya was working away tending the village gate, with Inari close by her side, she looked down the road and saw something a bit alarming. A stranger was approaching on horseback.

This stranger looked strikingly like the one she had encountered on her journey, which nearly killed Inari. The same kind of long and heavy duster, and thick-brimmed hat. That image would forever remain burned into her memory.

Inari smelled the stranger and bristled as he approached. Maya looked over at her friend to gauge her reaction. Inari didn't immediately jump into a fighting stance like she usually would when she sensed impending danger, but she was growling rather noticeably. Maya took this as a sign that the stranger likely didn't mean any harm, but there was still potential cause for concern. So, Maya placed her tools on the ground, drew her knife, and hid it behind her back as she waited for the stranger to approach.

A moment later, the stranger stopped his horse about twenty feet from where Maya was waiting, and he dismounted. Much to Maya's surprise, he was a short fellow.

"Hello there," said Maya, "how can I help you?"

"I'm looking for someone," replied the stranger.

"Oh yeah, who might that be?"

"Are you Maya, by any chance?"

"That depends. Who's asking?"

"I have something for her."

The stranger reached inside his duster. Out of pure instinct, Inari stood up, ready to pounce as Maya gripped her knife, ready to throw. After a moment of tension, the stranger pulled out his duster not a weapon, but a sealed letter.

"I have a message for Maya," said the stranger, "is that you?"

Both Maya and Inari calmed down and lowered their guard.

"Yes, that's me. Who is it from?"

"I was only instructed to deliver this message," he replied, "I wasn't told who sent it."

The stranger placed the message onto the ground and mounted his horse again.

"Wait," said Maya, "you're welcome to stay the night if you'd like."

"My instructions were to deliver this and leave," he replied, "nothing more."

And with that, the stranger rode away in a cloud of dust.

Once he was out of sight, Maya approached the sealed piece of paper lying on the ground and picked it up. On the face of the paper was an old-fashioned wax seal with her name handwritten underneath. Upon closer inspection, Maya could make out the shape of the seal. It was a single letter, "K."

Later that night, Maya sat inside her study, staring at the letter, with Inari resting at her feet. After taking a deep breath, Maya finally broke the seal, unfolded the paper, and read the hand-written letter.

Dear Maya,

I hope this letter finds you well. My thoughts have dwelled much on our last encounter. Your words struck something in me that I had not anticipated. For reasons I may never fully understand, your words gave me a sense of clarity I had not felt in a long time.

I still don't know if I am ready to believe in people's "better nature", as it were, but if there are more people like you out there, and I have not yet met them, it seems only right for me to try.

I have not shared the location of that place with anyone else, nor will I ever. I will continue to make the best out of the life I have been given. I will not come after you nor anyone you may care about. If you ever return to The Trade Post, you will be welcome as my friend.

Whether you choose to believe in my words or not, I may never know. I hope to share your dream of a better future for us all. I may not live to greet the next generation of travelers who will take your journey someday. I hope you will believe me when I say that if I am still around, and if you will permit me, I hope to become a part of it in some way.

Whatever else happens from here on out, know that I am still alive and more hopeful than ever because of you. I have seen your light, and I hope others will see it as well.

Your truly,
Kali

Maya was moved by Kali's letter in a way she hadn't expected. Had she helped someone reevaluate their stance on the world? Although Maya had no actual proof that any of what Kali had written was genuine, she felt in her heart that it must have been.

If we are to grow, we must have the courage to take the first step towards trusting one another again, she thought. *Maybe, this is the first step towards that glorious new future.*

After committing the letter to memory as best she could, Maya decided to burn it for safety. There must be no written discussion of the true nature of her journey. When the time was right, Maya knew she would have it all worked out for the next generation. Also, she would prepare for it a bit better than Dougie did.

After watching the paper fade away into ash, she and Inari were ready for bed. The two of them ventured upstairs to their bedroom. Maya had built a unique bed for Inari at the foot of hers.

As Inari jumped into her bed and prepared for a good night's sleep, Maya approached her workbench one more time. She opened a drawer and examined the old light bulb from her collection. As Maya gazed upon the small piece of glass and metal, she imagined the light she saw emanating from the machine within the bulb.

"Someday, when we're truly ready, maybe I'll get to see it lit up for myself."

Inari looked at Maya and tilted her head.

"Hey, I can dream, can't I?" Maya smiled and placed the old bulb back inside the drawer, put on her favorite nightshirt, and crawled into bed. Inari grabbed the blanket and pulled it over Maya before licking her face. Maya gently embraced her friend before looking deep into her dual-colored eyes.

"Goodnight, girl."

With that, Inari returned to her bed and curled up for the night. Maya soon followed suit and dozed off into a deep and comfortable sleep. She dreamed of her favorite memory with her mother…and her dual-colored eyes.

THE END

Appendix

The following is a collection of additional material (both scientific and creative) that will provide answers, explore possibilities, and expand the lore & mythology. Here you will find deleted chapters and original works intended to enrich the narrative and provide a scientifically sound basis for the story. Please enjoy all this content at your leisure.

Table of Contents:

The Science

SAM:
So, you see, the process of eliminating electricity and electrical power sounds impossible, but it's not. The real difficulty is eliminating only certain varieties of electrical power. Your brain and nervous system both rely on electricity, just as much as atomic bombs and refrigerators do.

MAE:
I would never have thought of that.

SAM:
Fortunately, electrical circuits created by biologic systems are similar but sufficiently different from electrical power transmissions to be easily distinguished. The ion channels in biological electric systems move at an incredibly slow velocity. Also, the formation of electrical potential, which makes electricity "flow," is different. In contrast,

the electrons "moving" along an ion channel of non-biologic systems as an electromagnetic wave, such as copper, move at about ninety percent of the speed of light, roughly 170,000-miles-a-second depending on the conductive quality of the metal. In contrast, biological transmissions are sluggish in comparison, roughly only 4-miles-a-second.

MAE:
Sam, I may have a degree in chaos theory, but that does not make me an expert in the electrical functions of the human brain.

SAM:
Think about it. If signals from your brain to your hands or legs arrived at the speed of light, you'd never drop anything or stumble. It's that fraction of a second it takes biological ions impulses to reach their destination that makes us so clumsy.

MAE:
So, your device slows down ions in the non-biologic electrical circuits, thus reducing the amount of power channeling to nearly nothing?

SAM:

Excellent hypothesis, but I'm afraid not. Biologic electricity travels at 0.002 percent of the velocity of non-biologic transmissions. This enormous difference allows my device to distinguish between biologic and nonbiologic electrical circuits easily and instantaneously. I can instruct the device to shut one down but not the other, even at remote distances and with literally multiple trillions of selections to make.

MAE:
But wait a moment! According to Einstein, matter and energy are equivalent to each other. So, what you're suggesting is impossible!

SAM:
Not quite. The idea that Einstein "proved" the equality of matter and energy is a mere myth. The matter isn't equivalent to energy, but rather mass is.

MAE:
Uh…the chaotician is stumped here!

SAM:
Let me put it this way: A brick is made up of matter. But brick is also mass and energy. If you warm up a brick in an oven, you

transfer energy to it. The matter stays the same, but the mass of the brick increases.

MAE:
Ah, much like the difference between, say, a wet sponge and a dry one.

SAM:
Exactly! The wet one is heavier than the other because its mass is more significant and thus is more influenced by the gravity well it's sitting in. The difference is that you can't "squeeze" the heat out of the brick to reduce its mass; you must let it sit for a while and radiate the heat, losing energy and thus mass. The MC2 thing in Einstein's formula is a mathematical result, a formula describing the real world but not a real-world event! With or without much mass, one tiny bit of matter contains immense amounts of energy if that matter is going at the velocity of light squared, which we know is not possible because the fastest anything in our universe can go the speed of light.

MAE:
But what's all this got to do with electricity?

SAM:

Your idea of slowing down the velocity of electrons in an electric circuit is imaginative, as you always are, but not possible. You see, that would involve some continuous force field to be applied globally and forever. That would be necessary because electrons will revert to their average velocity in the future, absent a continuous restraint. The Pulse from the Device must make an alteration that is permanent. See what I mean?

MAE:
That seems logical.

SAM:
Ahh, I see in your face that you're formulating another question in your mind. Fine. Electrical charges flow rapidly in non-biologic systems because the electrons in metals and other good conductors are delocalized. Unlike the electrons surrounding the nuclei of insulators, such as rubber or plastic, electrons in conductive materials are not associated or tightly bound to the atoms around which they orbit. With just a tiny energy boost, they leave the orbit of one nucleus and move on to an adjacent one. That's why the current moves. Current flows in one direction rather than randomly

are exciting but irrelevant to the device's function. So, I'll skip that part.

MAE:
That suits me just fine.

SAM:
To make the necessary permanent change, one must alter the "free spirit," as it were, of the electrons in metals. We need to bind them more closely to the specific neutron around which they orbit. This process does not alter the matter or the mass, or even the energy level of anything. Otherwise, there would be a violation of the laws of conservation of energy and mass. It is impossible to alter the total amount of mass and energy in a closed system. Our universe and thus our globe is part of a closed system.

MAE:
How is the device capable of altering such a fundamental characteristic of electrons?

SAM:
Just take my word for it. It does. The "how" is unknown even to me. I've been experimenting with electrons for decades. These experiments resulted in electrons in a copper sample becoming fixed to their

nuclei, blocking all electrical flow. The device is simply a much more powerful version of the machine that I'd recently built to perform my experiments. I claim no genius, only luck—sort of like an alchemist turning iron into gold after a couple of thousand tries.

MAE:
So, are you now going to show me how to turn this thing on if the time is ever right? I assume the device can, what you say, re-delocalize all the metallic electrons. Yes?

SAM:
Well, it's worked at a small scale here in the lab. I indeed assume it will function globally, both to localize and delocalize. If the Pulse localizes globally, there's no reason to believe it won't also delocalize if called upon to do so. Here, let me show you how to reset the control board. That part is straightforward.

Before The Wave

(The following summaries of events are selected from *Encycloquik®*, an online source chronicling a busy, distracted world, first posted in 2025. It was updated at the end of each month through April 30, 2037, ceasing publication on May 15, 2037. Their moto was, *Yesterday is History, Tomorrow's the Future™*)

<u>Years at a Glance</u>
<u>Summaries</u>

For details and additional events, see Main Text for each year

2025

On January 6, the 2024 presidential electoral vote count was: 133 for the Republican candidate, 136 for the Democratic candidate, and 269 for the Middle Majority candidate (270 being necessary to win). As it was about to vote to resolve this contingent election, the House was stormed by an armed mob of 9,437 discontented Republicans and Democrats. Unlike 2021, over half the Representatives were killed (232) and the remainder were held hostage for six days. The 203 Surviving Representatives were rescued by two battalions of Marines assigned to the Marine Corps Special Operations Command. All the insurrectionists were either killed or placed in military prisons. On January 13, the truncated House elected Middle Majority candidate to the office of the President by unanimous vote.

The second American Civil War started on January 18 and ended on July 14, after five months and 16 days of protracted fighting between and among hundreds of mutually antagonistic sociopolitical groups, police, and local/state governments on regional levels with the U.S. Defense Department ultimately restoring order by occupying all fifty states, President Byran Smallpockets (Middle Majority Party) having declared martial law on January 21. Given the amateurish combat skills of the regional civilian combatants, total national casualties were low at 503,346 (182,112 dead, 321234 wounded. Compare:

1,238,000 casualties during the First American Civil War). Martial law was terminated on August 17 when President Smallpockets assumed plenary control of the US Government under the Executive Emergency Control Act (EECA). His first decree ordered that Congress adjourn into indefinite recess.

The people and government of the United States being distracted by civil war, The People's Republic of China invaded and occupied Taiwan in February. Facing no resistance from NATO or the US. Russia occupied Moldova, Estonia, Latvia, Lithuania, Kazakhstan, Kyrgyzstan, Tajikistan, Turkmenistan, Uzbekistan, Armenia, Azerbaijan, Georgia, and Ukraine. Putin proclaimed the restoration of the USSR on June 5. China had remained neutral in exchange for Russian acquiescence to China's absorbing Outer Mongolia, restoring the Sino-Soviet borders of 1946.

On December 12, Pakistan's 6th and 8th Armored Divisions, supported by the entire 3rd Infantry Corps, invaded India but were halted after occupying only the western third of Kashmir. Hostilities continued along a stable front.

Accelerated Climate Change sent an estimated 9,467,000 refugees heading north and sound of the Equator, mostly into Turkey and eastern Europe from Africa and into the US from Central and Sound America. Global sea levels rose an unexpected 0.91 feet on average due to extreme calving of Antarctic glaciers, causing periodic flooding in low-lying coastal cities everywhere.

Global GDP declined by 8.2%.

2030

On January 31, by order of President Smallpockets, Federal troops were removed from the finally fully pacified pockets of lingering sociopolitical unrest in regions of Alabama, Arizona, Arkansas, Colorado, Georgia, Idaho, Kansas, Illinois, Missouri, Ohio, Pennsylvania, Texas, Maine, and northern California/Southern Oregon. Federal troops remained stationed in all 50 State Capitols. Congress remained in recess.

The Pakistan/India war remained in stalemate along the Kashmir frontlines. China and the USSR concluded an *Eternal Harmony Agreement* on May 1.

Sea levels rose 0.74 feet on average, causing massive costal evacuations initially estimated at 3,988,000. Climate Change and economic depression increased global migration by millions. More accurate estimates were still compiled by year's end sue to a general breakdown in governmental administration outside the US, China, and USSR.

Global GDP declined by 12.7%.

2036

The US experienced no major social disturbances in 2036. Federal troops remained stationed in all 50 State Capitals. On January 31, President Smallpockets announced that Congress, still in recess, would be dissolved forthwith. Federal elections for the newly constituted Legislative Branch, called *The Forum*, would be held on November 3, 2037. The Forum will act in an advisory capacity only, proposing legislation for Executive consideration. Administratively is to be under the supervision of the Department of Homeland Security; all candidates for office shall be selected by the President or his designees.

On May 29, Chairman Kim ordered a nuclear strike on Seoul, Tokyo, and Yokohama. Due to an apparent administrative error, the North Korean missile launch teams were provided the coded coordinates for a hypothetical strike on China. As a result, Beijing, Shanghai, and Guangzhou ceased to exist. A few minutes thereafter, the Yumen Chinese People's Liberation Army Missile Command in Gansu Province obliterated Pyongyang, Hamhung, and Chongjin. On August 11, to end the stalemate in Kashmir, Pakistan struck several cities in India with nuclear warheads, India retaliated. Total deaths in China, North Korea, India, and Pakistan estimated 52,000,000. Long term radiation casualties are still being determined. Extreme monsoon conditions over the Far East and Pacific mitigated global fallout consequences.

On December 8, Great Britain declared war on the EU due to the EU imposing a total economic blockade as sanctions against Britain's continued and continuous violations of the Brexit Accords. A repeat of the Phony War of 1939-40 was still holding at year's end.

On December 12, Iran launched a nuclear strike against Israel. Israel retaliated. Conditions in both countries are unknown due to a total absence of communications from either, extreme radiation levels preventing any reconnaissance from outside.

Sea levels rose an additional 0.83 feet, causing the evacuation of 1.3 billion people from coastal areas.

Global GDP declined by 38.1%.

2037
(Updated through April 30)

In early January, tensions rose between the USSR and the US, the only two major powers to have avoided nuclear attack and disruption during the last 8 months. The US suspected that Russia was planning to intervene in the still quiescent UK-EU war. On April 30, the US issued an ultimatum to the USSR that it withdraws its assembled armed forces from Russia's western border on the EU before May 15, 2037. No reply from the USSR to this ultimatum has been released.

On April 28, the CDC announced the appearance in Lebanon, Kansas of a new, extremely virulent virus (tentatively called COVID-omega/beta, but possibly an entirely new disease). Unspecified containment efforts are ongoing. Coincidentally, Lebanon is the geographic center of the contiguous U.S.

Annual sea level and GDP data are not yet available for this year.

The Natural Order

Excerpt from the admissions essay, *Mathematical Philosophy: A Different Study of Chaos Theory,* by Mae Douglass. Submitted for consideration July 4, 2018.)

As a child, one of my favorite things in life was the Calvin and Hobbes comic strip. A series about a young boy and his best friend who happens to be a stuffed Tiger and may or may not magically come to life, but only when unseen by others. My parents would read them to my brother and me almost every night. At that time, I was primarily entertained by their lovable and silly shenanigans. From pretending to land on Mars to blackmailing their babysitter with her science notes, there was nothing these two fortunate friends couldn't do. I was especially fond of how Hobbes would excitedly pounce his friend when he returned home from school, not unlike how my loving dogs would behave upon my arrival every day.

However, it wasn't until I grew older that I started seeing this comic strip in a completely different light. As I reread the comics in high school, I discovered something much deeper and profound that made me appreciate these characters and their fascinating introspectiveness a little more.

Of all the excellent and thought-provoking comic strips featuring Calvin and Hobbes, there's one that has always stood out to me. You can find it on pages 120-128 in the *10th Anniversary Book* published by the comics creator, Bill Watterson.

One day, while Calvin is enjoying himself on the swings during recess, he discovers from his part-time friend and part-time nemesis, Susie, a recess Baseball game organized for the kids. Most other children have signed up, but Calvin has no interest in organized sports, so he respectfully declines to join. Then, after prolonged, unwanted teasing and peer pressure, Calvin reluctantly signs up for the Baseball team and finds himself assigned to the outfield. After fighting boredom by pretending to be one of his many alter egos, Spaceman Spiff exploring an alien planet, Calvin suddenly hears the ball heading his way. With all his energy, he runs towards the ball and successfully catches it in his glove.

He rushes over to the other children expecting platitudes and congratulations; instead, he is bombarded with insults and anger, as it turns out he unintentionally caught the ball for the wrong team. Calvin expresses his confusion by proclaiming, "It's just a game! This is supposed to be fun!" To which one of the other children responds, "Games are only fun when you win! If you screw up again, you're dead meat, Calvin!" Disheartened by the toxic camaraderie, Calvin does the only sensible thing he can think of; he quits the team, but not after the coach refers to him as a quitter.

Later that day, Calvin meets with his best friend, Hobbes, and discusses the ridiculousness of the whole situation, leading the two of them to create probably one of the greatest games in the world, "Calvinball," the sport where the rules and methods are made up as you play.

From this little story, you may have surmised, the basis of my scientific & philosophical inquiry became distinct. While there are several topics this storyline contains and proves itself worthy of discussion (societal pressure vs. individualism, the necessity for unrestrained creativity, and so on), there is one idea I find myself most drawn to, and that is the nature of order & chaos.

We tend to view the two ideas as mutually exclusive most of the time, believing that one must be absent so the other may exist. In my humble and philosophical opinion, this is far from the truth. Order and chaos are not, and probably never have been, exclusive from one another. Instead, they are two sides of the same coin, or to phrase it another way, yin and yang.

Consider this ancient Chinese symbol. It represents dualism, balance, and, most pertinent to this essay, complementary forces. In most Eastern philosophies, it is widely believed that dueling factors, such as heat vs. cold or good vs. evil, require each other to function. To put it plainly, one cannot exist without the other. One may become more prominent than the other, but there can never be a complete absence, regardless of which side holds the most power or famous conjecture.

The very essence of life and civilization as we know it spawned from an act of chaos. When the asteroid struck our planet, it not only wiped out the dinosaurs (sadly), but it also forced all life on Earth to change. Because if there is one undeniable fact proven by that chunk of rock striking our little piece of Solar driftwood out-of-the-blue, it's that the Universe has no inherent sense of order. Therefore, chaos is the nature of existence.

This is not meant to imply that society and civilization are doomed to fail, far from it. It merely means that if society and civilization are to function correctly, we must abandon the illusion of control. Civilization does not function because it overcomes chaos; instead, we learn how to best move with the chaos. Those who succeed in finding the natural flow of existence live on to find new and remarkable discoveries of all kinds. In contrast, those who resist natural change remain trapped in a prison of their own making, unable to accept what must be done to survive.

Change is chaos, and order comes from accepting and adapting to the chaos. The sooner humanity accepts this as an undeniable fact, the better off we may become in the future. At least, that's just the humble opinion of one young woman applying for university.

Original Poetry
by
Zack Gibson

<u>The Dark is a Horrid Compass</u>

I've most likely stumbled down this

shadow infested street

Everything seemed so light though

I'm thankful I cannot be seen

In this nightmare-esque reality

abruptly ripped from a screen

I wish the innocent would quiet their

screams

Though they did eventually, not on

day one but day three

Lost City

What I wouldn't sacrifice to overlook

that enchanting city of lights again

Is exactly what I lost eternally when

everything was revoked

Now the only shimmers I'm honored

by are through the window beams

Go outside, lose your dreams

Clumpy Bark

A winding, crisp yet mossy oak

The merciless, antagonizing scratch

of the chilling winds

Drip-drops from the leaky pipes in

hardy filled sewers

Aromas of wild game, now neighbors

on the cackling flame

And charred meat to accompany

crickets in the near-dead night

That's how I know I'm still alive

<u>Self-Radio</u>
Hum what you what you recall 'cause
the radio ain't comin' back
Your jacket is your new skin, no need
for coat racks
We thank the sun for the warmth it
brings
Though strings were cut, a knife in
hand
Humming the tune to planetary
static

<u>Nature knew</u>
Thorns are but a warning
Rustling leaves are a warning
Sirens, alarms, barking, a heads-up

Where was my warning?

Last Call

Crazy? What's crazy?
When the world shatters like glass
and begins to get hazy
What is a life worth living without
people and things?
Is it truly crazy to still hear the
telephone ring?

A Haiku

Electric wasteland,
    Thank whomever for the kind sun
        It lets water run

Commissioned Illustrations

During the early phases of writing the book, I commissioned a talented artist named Jonathan Herzog to create the cover. While I was genuinely impressed with the illustration he provided, one of my editors suggested that the style didn't quite match the intended tone of the story. Plus, I had decided to redesign Maya's character model. Thus, I hired another equally talented artist, Rebecacovers, to create the existing cover.

Even so, I still wanted to include Jonathan's art in some capacity. So, when I decided to add the appendix, I asked Jonathan if he would like to draw a few extra illustrations to accompany the book. These are some of the pieces he created.

You can see more of Jonathan's art, including the original book cover, at his website:

https://www.jonherzogartist.com

Maya and Inari

You saved my life.

Making new friends.

I'm right here.

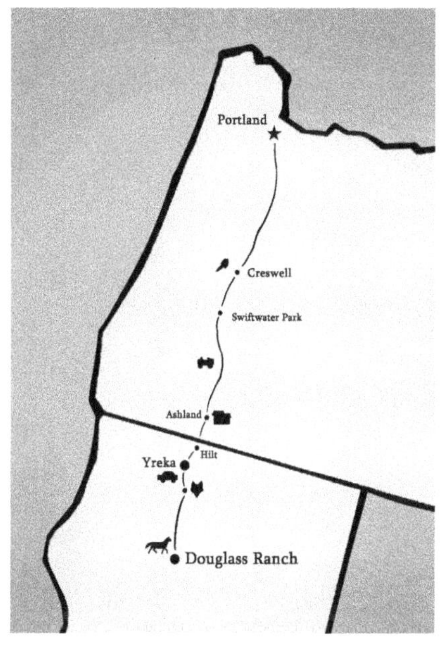

Maya's Journey